The Kangaroo Magic

LAKSHMAN CHAKRABORTY

Published by LAKSHMAN CHAKRABORTY, 2023.

THE KANGAROO MAGIC

First edition. September 11, 2023.

Copyright © 2023 LAKSHMAN CHAKRABORTY.

ISBN: 979-8223580591

Written by LAKSHMAN CHAKRABORTY.

Title

Kangaroo Magic

Story List

1. "Katie the Kangaroo's Jumping Adventure"
2. "Roxy and the Lost Joey"
3. "Kip the Kangaroo Learns to Hop"
4. "Joey's Big Day Out"
5. "Kangaroo Kate's Kangaroo Cake"
6. "Ricky the Roo's Rainy Day Adventure"
7. "Jump, Joey, Jump!"
8. "Kangaroo Kim's Surprise Party"
9. "Kangaroo Kevin and the Magic Pouch"
10. "Jenny's Jumpy Day"

11. "Kenny the Kangaroo's Kangaroo Parade"

12. "Sandy the Kangaroo's Soccer Game"

13. "Kylie's Kangaroo Capers"

14. "Roo-Roo's Amazing Adventure"

15. "Billy's Big Bounce"

16. "Kangaroo Kaitlyn and the Golden Leaf"

17. "Hoppy and His Secret Hideout"

18. "Kangaroo Kyle's Camping Trip"

19. "Ruby Roo's Rainbow Quest"

20. "Kipper's Kangaroo Art"

21. "Mia and the Mysterious Kangaroo Dance"

22. "Kangaroo Kristy's Space Adventure"

23. "Bouncing Benny's Birthday Surprise"

24. "Roxy Roo's Treasure Hunt"

25. "Kangaroo Kara's Cooking Chaos"

26. "Jake and the Kangaroo Kingdom"

27. "Katie and the Kangaroo Carnival"

28. "Rusty's Kangaroo Rescue"

29. "Kangaroo Kyle's Kite Festival"

30. "Joey and the Moonlight Magic"

31. "Jumping Jax's Jungle Journey"

32. "Kangaroo Kat's Colorful Crayons"

33. "Samantha's Secret Kangaroo Club"

34. "Kangaroo Ken's Kangaroo Caper"

35. "Daisy's Daring Kangaroo Dive"

36. "Kangaroo Kody's Kangaroo Castle"

37. "Zara's Zooming Kangaroo"

38. "Kangaroo Kate and the Kangaroo Choir"

39. "Holly's Kangaroo Holiday"

40. "Kip and the Kangaroo Olympics"

41. "Kangaroo Krista's Kangaroo Kingdom"

42. "Bobby and the Kangaroo Cup"

Katie the Kangaroo's Jumping Adventure

Once upon a time, in the heart of the Australian outback, lived a young kangaroo named Katie. He was a curious and adventurous kangaroo, always looking for exciting things to do. But there was one thing he loved more than anything else - jumping.

Katie was known far and wide for her incredible jumping skills. He could jump higher than any other kangaroo in the entire outback. His friends would often gather around to watch him in awe as he leaped across the open field.

One sunny morning, Katie wakes up with a burst of energy as the golden rays of the sun kiss the outside. He stretched his strong legs and said to himself, "Today is going to be a great day for jumping!" He got out of his cozy hole and walked over to his best friend Joey the wallaby. "Joey, do you want to come on a jumping adventure with me today?" Katie asked with a wink.

Joey, who like Katie loved adventure, enthusiastically agreed. "Of course, Katie! I can't wait to see where our jumping adventure takes us."

The two friends begin their adventure, hopping through the outback together. They jumped over bushes, jumped over streams, even ran with the wind. Katie's jumps were so high she could see the entire Outback in the air.

As they traveled deep into the outback, they came across a vast, rocky landscape. Katie and Joey stopped to admire the stunning rock formations, but they soon realized the rocks were too high to jump over.

Katie frowned, confused. "How can we continue our adventure with these tall rocks in our way?"

Joey, always quick to think, suggested, "Maybe we could climb the rocks instead of jumping over them!"
So, Katie and Joey start climbing the rocky mountain. It was tough, but they were determined to reach the top. At every step, they encouraged each other and soon they stood triumphantly at the summit, gazing at the breathtaking view.
Their adventures continued as they explored the rocky terrain, discovering hidden caves and sparkling gems. They even befriended a curious lizard named Lizzie who lived among the rocks.
As the day goes on, Katie and Joey's jumping adventure leads them to a beautiful waterfall. Katie couldn't resist the urge to jump into the cool, refreshing water. With a graceful leap, he plunged into the pool below, splashing water everywhere.
Joey joined in, and they spent hours swimming and playing in the sparkling pool. It was a perfect way to end their incredible adventure.
As the sun began to set, Katie and Joey decided it was time to head home. They came back through the outback and shared stories and laughs.
When they finally reached their hole, they were exhausted but filled with joy. Katie understood that adventures can be found in the most unexpected places and that sometimes, you don't need to jump high to have a great time.
Happy, they bid their farewells, promising more adventures together. Katie the kangaroo went to sleep that night, dreaming of the next jumping adventure that awaited her.
And so, in the vast and beautiful Australian outback, Katie the kangaroo hops and bounds to explore, because there are always

new and exciting adventures just waiting to be discovered by a kangaroo with a love for jumping.

Roxy and the Lost Joey

Once upon a time in the vast and sunny outback of Australia, there lived a young kangaroo named Roxy. Roxy was an adventurous and curious kangaroo who loved to explore beautiful landscapes with her friends. He had a loving family with his mother, father and a younger brother named Joey.

One bright morning, Roxy and Joey wake up early, excited for their day of adventure. They decide to go to a nearby eucalyptus forest with their friends Benny the Koala and Lila the Kookaburra. They all gathered at the edge of the forest, ready for their fun-filled day.

"Let's play thief!" Roxy suggested, her eyes blazing with excitement. Everyone agreed, and Benny began counting while the others ran off to find a hiding place. Roxy found a perfect spot behind a bush, but when Benny finished counting and started searching, there was no sign of Joey.

They searched high and low, jumped on logs, and called Joey's name, but he was nowhere to be found. Panic sets in, and Roxy's heart races.

"Where could he be?" Roxy whispered to herself worriedly.

Benny, Lila and Roxy decide to split up to cover more ground. They searched all morning, calling out for Joey, but there was no response. As the day wore on, Roxy's anxiety grew, and tears welled up in her eyes.

They were all feeling tired and scared as the sun started to set. Roxy couldn't bear the thought of Zoar being alone in the dark forest. He climbed a hill, hoping to get a better vantage point. From there he saw something familiar in the distance.

It was Joey's favorite tree, with its hollow trunk where he liked to sleep. Roxy's heart raced as she approached it, her hope rekindled. And there, inside the hollow trunk, was little Joey, safe and sound, but fast asleep.

Roxy let out a squeal of pleasure and gently woke Joey up. He blinked, "Roxy, time to go home?"

"Yes, Joey, it's time," she replied, relief flooding over her.

He scooped up his younger brother in his strong arms, and together they walked back to where their friends were waiting anxiously. Benny and Leela cheered as they saw Joey safe and sound.

"Thank God, you're all right, Joey!" Benny exclaimed, as he was hugged by a large koala.

Roxy smiled, feeling grateful that her little brother was safe. "I'm sorry, Joey. I should have kept a closer eye on you."

Joey hugged Roxy tightly. "Okay, sis. I've learned my lesson too. I shouldn't have wandered off."

On their way home, the setting sun paints the sky in shades of orange and pink. Roxy and Joey walked side by side, their hearts full of love for each other and their friends. They realized that even in the most terrifying times, their family and friends would always be there to help and support them.

And so, Roxy, Joey, Benny and Lila continue their adventure in the Australian outback, knowing that as long as they stick together, they can overcome any challenge that comes their way. The bonds of friendship and family were their greatest treasures, and they cherished them every day.

Kip the Kangaroo Learns to Hop

Once upon a time in the vast and beautiful Australian outback, there lived a young kangaroo named Kip. Kip was not like other kangaroos; He could not jump like them. Every day, he watched his friends leap when he could only take small, clumsy steps.

Kip felt sad and went out. He would sit by the old gum tree and watch his friends play hopscotch and jump over rocks. They would run and jump high into the air while Kip could only watch, his feet barely lifting off the ground.

One sunny morning, Kip decides he's had enough. He wanted to learn how to hop like his kangaroo friends. He jumped on his mother, Mama Roo, who was sunbathing nearby (in her own clumsy way).

"Mama," said Kip, "I want to learn how to jump like the other kangaroos. Can you teach me?"

Mama Roo smiled, "Of course, Kip! Hopping is what we kangaroos do best. But it takes practice and patience. Are you ready to try it?"

Kip nodded eagerly. He was determined to learn how to jump.

Mama Roo started by showing Kip the basics. He explained, "Start with your knees bent, just like this, and then push off the ground with your back foot. Use your tailbone for balance. It might feel weird at first, but with practice, you'll get the hang of it."

Kip tried to copy his mother's movements, but he stumbled and fell. He tried again and again, but it seemed that hooping was much harder than it looked. He is about to give up when Mama Roo encourages him to keep trying.

"Remember, Kip," said Mama Roo, "every kangaroo was once a beginner. You get better with practice."

Kip didn't give up. He practiced jumping every day. Sometimes he jumps short distances, sometimes he jumps in place. He even practiced running the stick over small sticks and stones. It was hard work, and his legs hurt, but he was determined to learn.

Weeks passed, and Kip's hopping began to improve. He can go a little higher and a little farther every day. His friends, who had been cheering him on all along, cheered him on.

One sunny afternoon, there was a special kangaroo hopping competition in the outback. Kip decided it was time to put his new skills to the test. He joined his friends on the run, and the other kangaroos watched with excitement.

The race began, and Kip jumped with all his might. He pushed off the ground, used his tail for balance, and flew into the air. His friends were amazed at how far and how high Kip could climb. He was no longer the kangaroo who could not jump; He was Kip, the kangaroo who learned to jump!

In the end, Kip didn't win the race, but he didn't mind at all. He achieved something more important he learned to jump, and he gained the confidence to try new things.

From that day on, Kip knew that with determination and practice, he could achieve anything he set his mind to. And he was the happiest kangaroo in the outback, knowing that he had found his own special way to breeze through life.

And so, the story of Keep the Kangaroo teaches us that with perseverance and the support of loved ones, we can overcome challenges and achieve our goals, no matter how impossible they may seem at
first.

Joey's Big Day Out

Once upon a time in the vast outback of Australia, there lived a young kangaroo named
Joey. Joey was an energetic little kangaroo, full of curiosity and energy. He lived in a cozy pouch inside his mother's belly, feeling safe and snug, but he dreamed of the day he would have his big adventure.
One sunny morning, Joey's mother, Mama Roo, decided it was time for Joey to see the world outside his pouch. He jumped over to Joey, nudged him gently and said, "Today, my dear Joey, it's time for your big day."
Joy's heart raced with excitement. He got out of Mama Roo's pouch and stretched his little legs. The world around him was vast and beautiful, golden fields of grass as far as he could see.
Mama Roo gave Joey some important advice. "Joey, listen carefully. Always stay close to me, and never wander too far. The outback can be a wild and unpredictable place."
Zoe nodded, eager to explore. They began their adventure, leaping through the tall grass, and Joey's eyes widened when he saw the colorful bird flying overhead and heard the kookaburra's laugh in the distance.
When they jumped, they met a wise old emu named Emma. He had long legs and soft feathers like clouds. Emma told Joey and Mama Roo about the different animals and plants of the Outback. Joey was fascinated by the story and the vastness of the land.
Their journey continued, and they encountered a group of wallabies playing a game of hide and seek. Joey joined in the fun, hopping and

bouncing with his new friends. He felt like he was flying, and he couldn't stop laughing.

After a while, Mama Roo gently reminded Joey, "It's time to move on, Joey. We still have more to see." Joey said goodbye to his wallaby friends and headed back to Mama Roo.

They ventured deeper into the outback, where they found a waterhole under the sun. Joey was curious and wanted to take a sip, but Mama Roo warned him, "Always check with me before you do anything, Joey."

They reached the waterhole, and Mama Roo carefully checked the water to make sure it was safe. Joey took a small drink, feeling refreshed and grateful for his mother's wisdom.

As the sun set, Mama Ru took Joey to a peaceful place where they could rest for the night. Under the starry outback sky, Mama Roo told Joey stories of their ancestors and their adventures.

Joey lives close to Mama Roo, feeling safe and loved. He realizes that while the world is big and exciting, there is no place like home and the warmth of his mother's pouch.

Dreaming of more adventures ahead, Joey closed his eyes and fell asleep, knowing that every day in the outback was a big day filled with love, learning, and new friends.

And so, Joey's big day was not just a journey through the outback but a journey of discovery, love and bonding between a young kangaroo and his wise and caring mother.

Kangaroo Kate's Kangaroo Cake

Once upon a time, in the heart of the Australian outback, there lived a young kangaroo named Kangaroo Kate. Kate was a lively and creative kangaroo who loved two things more than anything in the world: baking and kangaroos.

One sunny morning, Kate wakes up with an idea that excites her. She decided she would bake a special cake, not just any cake, but a kangaroo cake! Kate believed her cake could bring joy to all the kangaroos in the Outback. But there was one small problem - Kate had never baked a cake before.

Determined to make her dream come true, Kate turns to her friend Walter the wombat, who is known for his cooking skills. He asked Walter for help and he gladly agreed.

Together, they gathered all the ingredients they needed: flour, sugar, eggs, and a dash of outback magic.

Kate was the first to crack the egg and it wasn't as easy as it looked. The eggshells all flew away, but they laughed and tried again. Walter showed Kate how to mix the batter until it W as just right. Kate loved the feel of the dough between her paws as she mixed and mixed.

As the cake baked in the oven, the delicious smell filled Kate's little scent. She couldn't wait to share her kangaroo cake with all her kangaroo friends. Walter, being a kind friend, offered to help decorate the cake. They use berries to make a kangaroo shape on top and make it look like a kangaroo party.

When the cake was finally ready, Kate invited all her kangaroo friends over for a surprise.

They all gathered in front of his burrow, their tails wagging in excitement. Kate brought out the kangaroo cake and gasps of surprise filled the air.

"Wow! It's a kangaroo cake!" shouted Joey Jim, the youngest kangaroo in the group.

Kate smiled happily. "I made this just for you all because I love kangaroos and wanted to celebrate our unique outback family!"

The kangaroos could not believe their eyes. They each took a piece of the cake and tasted it. It was the most delicious cake they had ever eaten and it filled their hearts with warmth.

As they enjoyed their cake, they realized that what made the cake truly special was the love and effort Kate put into making it. It wasn't just a cake; It was a symbol of their friendship and their love for each other.

Since that day, Kangaroo Kate's Kangaroo Cake has become a tradition in the Outback. Every year, she would bake a new kangaroo cake to celebrate their unique bond and the beauty of their home.

And so, Kangaroo Kate's dream to bring joy to all the kangaroos of the outback came true, not because of a fancy cake, but because of the love and unity it represented.

The kangaroos jumped and danced, their hearts full of joy and Kate realized that the best things in life were not always things but the love and friendship they shared. And that, my dear friends, is the sweetest lesson of all.

Ricky the Roo's Rainy Day Adventure

Once upon a time in the vast and sunny land of Australia lived a young kangaroo named

Ricky. Ricky was a cheerful and adventurous kangaroo who loved to explore the beautiful outback with his friends. However, one day, something unusual happened - it started raining, and it didn't seem like it would stop anytime soon.

Riki looked up from his cozy pouch and frowned. "What a sad day," he thought, feeling disappointed that he couldn't play outside with his friends. His mother, Mrs. Ru, noticed his gloom and said, "Don't worry, Ricky. Rainy days can be fun too. Let's make the most of it!"

Mrs. Roo had an idea. He opened his pouch, revealing a pile of colorful, shiny, and magical buttons. "These are my special buttons," she said with a smile. "Each button can take us on a different adventure, even on a rainy day!"

Riki's eyes sparkled with excitement. He chose a button that shone like the sun. With a push, the rain outside turned into a magical waterfall. They were in a lush rainforest full of vibrant flowers and curious animals. Riki could not believe his eyes!

"Wow, Mom! That's amazing!" Ricky exclaimed as he wandered around, exploring the rainforest. He met a friendly parrot who taught him how to imitate its cheerful chirping. Ricky practiced and soon sounded like his new friend.

After a while Ricky pressed another button. It transformed the room into a sandy beach.

The rain became waves crashing on the shore, and seagulls filled the air with their soothing calls. Ricky built sand castles and splashed in the imaginary sea. It was just like a summer vacation at home!

As the day went on, Ricky and his mother pushed more buttons. They soared with colorful birds, swam with playful dolphins and even ventured deep into the Great Barrier Reef.

Ricky learns about all the incredible places Australia has to offer from the comfort of his backpack.

But as the day grew darker, Ricky felt a little tired. Mrs. Roo noticed and suggested a final adventure. He pressed a button that transformed their cozy pod into a nocturnal wonderland. The stars twinkled overhead, and the soothing sounds of the bushes filled the air.

"Mom, it's been the best rainy day ever!" Ricky said, laying down next to his mother in their cozy sack.

Mrs. Ru smiled and hugged him lovingly. "Sometimes, the most magical adventures happen at home, Ricky."

Ricky nodded, feeling grateful for his mother and the wonderful day they had shared. As the rain continued to fall outside, he fell asleep, dreaming of future adventures in his heart.

And so, Ricky the Roo's rainy day adventure turns into a day full of excitement, learning and love, reminding him that even on the darkest days, there is always sunshine in the heart. the end

Jump, Joey, Jump!

Once upon a time in the vast outback of Australia, there lived a young kangaroo named

Joey. Joey was a bright and adventurous kangaroo who loved to explore the world around him. But there was one thing he dreamed of more than anything else - he wanted to jump higher than any kangaroo had jumped before.

Joey spent his days walking around, trying to jump higher with each jump. He watched the older kangaroos in awe, marveling at their leaps. "I want to jump like them one day," she said to herself.

One sunny morning, while Joey was practicing his jumps, he met an old and wise kangaroo named Kip. Kip had seen a lot of kangaroos in his time and could tell that Joey was determined to achieve something special. Kip turned to Joey and said, "Young man, I see you have a dream. What do you want to achieve?"

Joey's eyes lit up, and he replied, "I want to jump higher than any kangaroo has jumped before! I want to touch the sky with my feet!" Kip smiled kindly at Joey's enthusiasm. "It is a wonderful dream, my dear friend," he said. "But to jump high, you must first learn to jump smart. Come with me; I'll teach you the secret."

Joey followed the keep to a quiet part of the outback with tall trees and soft, sandy soil.

Kip began to explain the mystery to Joey. "To jump high, you need to use your leg power wisely. Bend your knees a little more and push off the ground with all your strength."

Joey listened attentively and immediately began practicing. He bent his knees a little more and pushed off the ground as hard as he could. At first, his jumps were a bit shaky, but he continued to improve with each attempt.

Days turned into weeks, and Joey practiced diligently under Kip's guidance. He became stronger and more skilled day by day. He even developed a special trick of his own - he would swing his long tail like a pendulum to keep his balance higher in the sky.

One sunny afternoon, Joey felt ready to put his newfound skills to the test. He invited all the kangaroos of the outback and watched him jump. Everyone gathered around, curious to see what Joey had learned.

Taking a deep breath, Joey bent his knees, wagged his tail, and launched himself into the air. He rose higher and higher, almost touching the leaves of the tall trees. The crowd gasped as Joey's dream came true - he jumped higher than any kangaroo had jumped before! Joey gracefully returned to the ground to the cheers and applause of his fellow kangaroos. He felt proud of himself, not only for his incredible jump but also for the hard work and determination he put in to achieve his dream.

From that day on, Joey's jumping skills became legendary in the Australian outback. He taught young kangaroos the secrets of high jumping, just as Kip had taught him.

And so, the story of Joey, the kangaroo who learned to jump higher, became an inspiration to all kangaroos out there. It taught them that with hard work, determination and a little guidance, they could reach for the stars and make their dreams come true.

Kangaroo Kim's Surprise Party

Once upon a time, in the heart of the Australian outback, lived a young kangaroo named Kim. Kim was known for her boundless energy and bouncy spirit like her jumps. He had a big heart and was always helping his friends.

One sunny morning, while walking around the eucalyptus tree, Kim noticed a sad look on her friend Joey's face. Joey was a small kangaroo who had recently moved to the outback. He missed his old home and his friends terribly.

"What's wrong, Joey?" Kim asked, concerned.

"I miss my old friends back in town," Joey replied. "I used to have amazing surprise parties with them."

Kim's eyes lit up with a thought. "I know what will make you happy, Joey! We'll give you the best surprise party ever!"

Joy's face lit up with hope. "You'll do it for me, Kim?"

"Absolutely!" Kim exclaimed, and they immediately began planning. They decide to invite all their friends from the outback and make it a day to remember.

Kim, as the organizer, took charge of making the colorful invitations, while Joey helped with the decorations. They hung balloons from gum trees, set the table with delicious eucalyptus leaf sandwiches, and prepared berry juice in giant leaf cups.

The day of the party arrived, and the excitement was palpable. Kim and Joey's friends arrive one by one. There was Benny the wallaby, Rosie the kookaburra and Tommy the platypus, to name a few.

The moment had come. Kim took Joey to the clearing in the woods where they would set up the party. Joy's eyes widened as she saw the decorations, heard the laughter of friends and smelled the delicious food. "Is this all for me?" she asked, tears of joy welling up in her eyes. Kim nodded and smiled. "Welcome to your surprise party, Joey!"

The party was a huge success. They played games like "Hopscotch Hurdles" and "Eucalyptus Leaf Toss". Everyone had a fantastic time, especially Joey. He laughed, jumped and made new friends. It was a day filled with happiness and love.

As the sun sank below the horizon, they gathered around the campfire and sang. The burning flames created a warm and cozy atmosphere. Joe feels like he's found a new family in the Outback.

When it was time to say goodbye, Joy had tears in her eyes again, but this time they were tears of gratitude. "Thank you, Kim, for the most amazing surprise party ever. I don't miss my old home anymore because I have wonderful friends like you."

Kim hugged Zoya tightly. "You're welcome, Joey. We're a family now, and families stick together. You'll never be alone."

From that day on, Joey became a cherished member of the Outback community. She and Kim were best friends, and they continued to host surprise parties for others who needed a little extra love and cheer.

And so, in the heart of the Australian outback, where kangaroos pounced, wallabies bounded, and kookaburras laughed, bonds of friendship grew stronger with each passing day. Kangaroo Kim's surprise party not only brought joy to Joey but also filled their hearts with the warmth of togetherness.

The End

Kangaroo Kevin and the Magic Pouch

Once upon a time, in the heart of the Australian outback, there lived a young kangaroo named Kevin. Kevin was unlike any other kangaroo because he had a very special pouch, unlike the regular pouches of kangaroos. Her pouch was magic!

One sunny morning, as Kevin wandered around, he found his kangaroo friends playing by a sparkling creek. They were jumping and splashing in the water. Kevin wanted to join the fun, but he couldn't swim because of his magical pouch. You see, whenever Kevin gets wet, his pouch starts to glow with a soft, mysterious light.

Curious about his magical pouch, Kevin decides to visit his wise old friend, the wise wallaby Walter, who lives in a cozy burrow nearby.

"Hello, Kevin," Walter greeted him with a warm smile. "What brings you here today?"

Kevin explains his plight about the magic pouch and how it prevents him from playing in the water. Walter listened intently, his mind struck by the shock. Then, he said, "Kevin, your bag is not a burden; it's a gift! But gifts often come with responsibility."

Kevin looked surprised. "What do you mean, Walter?"

Walter explained, "Your magical pouch has the power to protect the land and its creatures.

Whenever it lights up, it means that you need to do something important. It's a call to action."

Kevin's eyes widened in excitement. "What should I do, Walter?"

Walter smiled. "First, you must follow your gut. Let it guide you to where you need it most."

With renewed purpose, Kevin thanked Walter and left. As he followed the glowing pouch, it led him deep into the heart of the outback. On the way, he encounters needy creatures. He helped a lost kangaroo find its way home, shared his meals with a hungry koala and even gave a sad emu a comforting hug.

Every time Kevin's sac lit up, he felt a warm feeling of fulfillment and happiness. She realized that helping others was the most magical thing she could do.

One day, Kevin's pouch starts to glow brighter than ever. This led him to a dry and dusty area of the outback where a group of thirsty animals gathered around an empty waterhole. The animals were desperate for water and Kevin knew he had to help them.

With a stern look on his face, Kevin jumped into the nearest creek, filled his pouch with water, and then turned to the thirsty creatures.

As he released the water from his pouch, it flowed like a river, quenching the animals' thirst.

The animals cheered and thanked Kevin for his kindness. His pouch glowed brighter, indicating his most important task yet - bringing water to dry land.

From that day on, Kangaroo Kevin became known as the hero of the Outback. He continued to use his magical pouch to help those in need and his heart swelled with joy.

And so, Kangaroo Kevin learned that true magic was not in his pouch but in the love and kindness he shared with others. And this, dear children, is the story of Kevin the Kangaroo and the Magic Pouch—the story of a kangaroo who discovered that the greatest magic was the magic of giving and caring for those in need.

Jenny's Jumpy Day

Once upon a time in the vast and sunny Australian outback, lived a young kangaroo, Jenip. Jenny was known for her incredible jumping buddy. He can jump with much more pressure than his old counterparts, and his friends love nothing more than his jumps.

A bright and bouncy long, Jenny extra lullaby normalises sleep. He fell from his rucksack, ready for an adventure. He makes a cozy den among the eucalyptus trees with his mother, father and younger brother Joey.

"Good morning, Mom! Good morning, Dad! Good morning, Joey!" Jenny chirped as she considered her family.

"Good morning, Jenny," her mother said with a loving smile. "What are you so excited about today?"

"I don't know, Mom," Jenny replied. "I think today should be written as a special day for jumping!"

Patting Jay affectionately on the back, his father said, "Well then, go and have a jolly day, just mind the food my dear."

Jenny promises to be careful and bounds out of the hole. He glimpsed the golden outback power, his long, and propelled him into the air. His first stop was at his friend Ricky's place. "Hi, Jenny!" Ricky greeted him with a friendly wave. "What's up?"

"I'm having a day! How high can I jump?" cried Jenny.

Riki's face lit up with excitement. "Absolutely!"

Jenny took a few steps back, crouched down, then, with all her might, she leaped into the air. He rose further into the sky and for a moment seemed to touch. Ricky marvels at Jenny's amazing leap into a new high school promotion.

"That was incredible, Jenny!" Ricky cheered.

Jenny smiled. "Thanks, Ricky! It was a jump day as I call it energy!"

Two friends spent the morning jumping and laughing. As the sun rose high in the sky, Jenny went to visit her friend Rosie, who lived by a sparkling stream.

"Hey Rosie!" Jenny called as she climbed the stream.

Rosie was preoccupied with her hopping, but she let Jenny know about it. "Hello, Jenny! What's up here?"

"I've had a day! Jenny gave the page."

Rosie's eyes glow with excitement, and she agrees to the vote. Jenny and Rosie lined up in the stream, and the three of them were off. They leaped and leaped to the banks of their stream.

The race was neck-and-neck, but in the end, Jenny was able to edge out Rosie for a lizardy finish. They burst into laughter by the stream, their hearts filled with joy.

As the days go by, Jenny meets more friends and shares her wild adventures. He ran with Benny, danced with Kailyn and even helped Kyle with his jumping.

As the sun began to sink into the horizon, Jenny made her way home, her heart full. He commented that having a rough day wasn't just about his opinion; It was about sharing moments of laughter, joy and pure fun with his friends.

"Mom, dad, I'm back!" Jenny called as she returned to her den.

His family gathered around him, to hear about his jumpy day. Jenny regaled them with stories of her adventures, and they witnessed her tortures.

With Jenny night and its comfortable pouch, you can cheer up what could be a stormy day, live a happy heart with your genius friends.

And so, in her warm pouch, Jenny went to sleep, looking forward to the next adventure.

the end

Kenny the Kangaroo's Kangaroo Parade

Once upon a time, in the heart of the Australian outback, there lived a young kangaroo named Kenny. Kenny was a friendly and curious kangaroo with a unique dream – he wanted to organize the most amazing kangaroo parade ever seen.

Kenny lived in a cozy den with his family. He shared his dream with his parents, who were supportive and encouraging. His mother, Kathy, said, "That sounds like a great idea, Kenny! But organizing the parade is a big job. You're going to need help."

Kenny nodded in agreement. He knew that planning the parade would not be easy. So, he goes to his best friends Buro - Ruby the kangaroo, Benny the koala and Sammy the wombat - to share his idea.

Ruby, Benny and Sammy were excited about the idea of a kangaroo parade. They agree to help Kenny, each using their unique talents. Ruby was great at making colorful banners and flags. Benny knew how to play the trumpet, and Sammy was great at organizing events.

Their first task was to set a date for the parade. After much discussion, they chose a sunny Saturday two weeks away. They decided to call it "Kenny's Kangaroo Parade" and word quickly spread across the Outback.

Kenny and his friends begin working tirelessly to plan their parade. Ruby has created stunning banners with vibrant colors that can be seen from miles away. Benny practiced his trumpet skills and composed a catchy tune for the parade. Sammy took charge of organizing food stalls, games and rides for everyone after the parade.

As the day of the parade approached, excitement filled the air. Kangaroos and other animals from all over the outback began to gather. They all wanted to be part of Kenny's special parade. Finally, the big day has arrived. The sun shone brightly in the sky and the air was filled with laughter and music. Kenny, Ruby, Benny, and Sammy proudly led the parade, walking down the parade route with smiles on their faces. Kenny couldn't believe his dream had come true. Kangaroos of all shapes and colors display their unique talents in the parade. Some kangaroos danced, some played musical instruments and others did amazing tricks. The crowd cheered and applauded as they watched the spectacle.

After the parade, the Outback turns into a carnival of joy and fun. There were delicious eucalyptus leaf pies, bouncy kangaroo rides and even a kangaroo painting booth where kids could decorate their own pouches. The atmosphere was filled with joy and laughter.

Kenny couldn't be happier. His dream of organizing a kangaroo parade not only came true but also brought his friends and the entire Outback community together.

Kenny gathers his friends around as the sun begins to set. He thanks Ruby for her beautiful banner, Benny for his catchy parade tune, and Sammy for organizing the carnival. "I couldn't have done it without all of you," he said gratefully.

Kenny's Kangaroo Parade became an annual event that brought joy and unity to the Australian outback. Kenny's dream not only came true but also created lasting memories for all.

And so, under the twinkling stars of the Outback, Kenny and his friends knew that dreams, no matter how big, could be achieved with the help of loved ones and a little determination.

Since that day, Kenny's Kangaroo Parade has become a symbol of friendship, unity and the power to chase your dreams. And Kenny, the kangaroo with big dreams, runs through life, spreading joy wherever he goes.

Sandy the Kangaroo's Soccer Game

Once upon a time, in the heart of the Australian outback, lived a young kangaroo named

Sandy. Sandy was a bubbly and energetic kangaroo who loved to jump around, but most of all, she loved playing soccer with her friends. Every afternoon, Sandy and his kangaroo

friends would gather in a dusty field near a eucalyptus tree for a friendly game of soccer.

Sandy's soccer team was called the "Outback Kickers" and was known around for their speed and teamwork. They were a tight-knit group of kangaroos who always had a blast on the field.

One sunny afternoon, as Sandy and her friends gather for their game, they notice a new kangaroo that seems a little lonely. His name is Joey, and he's just moved to the outback from far away. Sandy, the friendly and kind kangaroo that she was, introduced herself to Joey by bonding.

"Hi, I'm Sandy! Would you like to join our soccer game?" she asked with a warm smile.

Joey hesitated a moment, feeling a little shy in all the new faces. But Sandy's kindness makes him feel welcome, and he agrees to join the Outback Kickers.

The game begins, and Sandy is thrilled to have a new friend on her team. He passed the ball to Joey, who showed some impressive

dribbling skills. The other Kangaroos were amazed by Joey's talent and quickly realized that he was a valuable addition to their team.
As the game wore on, the Outback Kickers played their hearts out. Sandy and Joey formed a great pair, passing the ball back and forth, evading the opposition and scoring with grace. Their teamwork was unbeatable, and they soon found themselves leading the game.
But as the game wore on, the opposing team, the "Bush Blazers," began to play more aggressively. They were determined to catch up. The tension in the air was palpable as the clock ticked down.
At the last moment, with the score tied, it was a game win over Sandy and Joey. Sandy passed the ball to Joey, who raced past the Bush Blazers defenders down the field. With a swift kick, Joey sends the soccer ball flying toward the goal.
Goal! The Kangaroos crowd erupted in cheers as the soccer ball found the back of the net. Sandy and Joey did it! They won the game for the Outback Kickers.
The Bush Blazers congratulated the Outback Kickers on their amazing win, and even though they lost, they couldn't help but smile at the incredible teamwork and sportsmanship they witnessed.
Not only did Sandy and Joey win the game, they also won the hearts of their fellow kangaroos. Joey felt like he finally found a place where he belonged and Sandy not only

made a new friend but also learned the importance of welcoming newcomers graciously.

From that day on, Sandy, Joey, and the Outback Kickers played soccer together every afternoon, and their friendship grew stronger with each game. They showed everyone that when you work together and welcome new friends with open arms, you can achieve anything.
And so, the Outback becomes a happier place, filled with the joyous sounds of kangaroos playing football and making memories that will last a lifetime.

Kylie's Kangaroo Capers

Once upon a time, in the vast outback of Australia, there lived a little girl named Kylie.

He was an adventurous and curious child who loved to explore the wilderness that surrounded his family's farm. But what Kylie loved the most was the kangaroo. The sight

of these majestic animals leaping across the open plain filled him with wonder and awe.

One sunny morning, Kylie decided to embark on a great adventure. He puts on his favorite explorer hat, packs a small bag with snacks and his trusty binoculars, and heads out into the wilderness. His goal? See the kangaroos up close and personal.

Heading deep into the outback, Kylie kept her eyes peeled for any sign of kangaroos. He watched the long grass sway in the wind, hoping to catch a glimpse of those vague

whooping figures. After what felt like hours, he saw a crowd of kangaroos in the distance.

Excitement bubbled up inside him, and he moved closer, trying not to scare them. Kylie's heart fluttered with every step she took. He was almost there when, unexpectedly, he tripped over a tree root and fell to the ground. The kangaroos scurried away in a flash, and Kylie was dismayed.

But Kylie was not one to give up easily. He dusted himself off and decided to try a different approach. He remembered his grandmother's old stories about the bush and how sometimes kangaroos came to drink at the water hole. With determination in her eyes, Kylie sets off in search of a watering hole.

Moments later, Kylie spotted a beautiful water hole between two towering eucalyptus trees. He settled down quietly, hid behind a rock and waited patiently. It didn't take long for a kangaroo to cautiously approach the watering hole.

Kylie's heart raced, but she remained still as a statue. He watched in awe as the kangaroo bent down to drink, its long tail wagging gracefully. Through her binoculars Kylie could see the kangaroo's soft, brown fur and those big, expressive eyes. It was a moment she would never forget.

As she sat there, Kylie noticed something unusual. The kangaroo appears to be twitching, and its paw is injured. His adventurous spirit has now turned into a caring one. He knew he had to help this kangaroo.

Slowly, Kylie approached the injured kangaroo, her heart full of compassion. He gently reached out and touched her soft fur. The kangaroo looked up at him with those big, trusting eyes. Carefully, Kylie made a makeshift bandage for the injured paw using her spare shirt and some clean water from her canteen.

Days turned into weeks as Kylie cared for injured kangaroos. He named his new friend

Roo-Roo. Together, they explore the outback, but this time Kylie doesn't need binoculars to see kangaroos up close. He had a real-life kangaroo friend by his side.

In time, Roo-roo's paw heals and she regains her strength. Kylie knew it was time to release her into the wild where she belonged. With a heavy heart, Kylie said goodbye to her dear friend.

As she watched Roo-Roo go into the wilderness, Kylie felt a sense of accomplishment.

Not only did he fulfill his dream of seeing kangaroos up close, he also made a lifelong friend in the process. From that day on, he knew that adventures in the outback would always hold wonderful surprises, especially when you least expect them.

Roo-Roo's Amazing Adventure

Once upon a time in the vast and colorful Australian outback, there lived a little kangaroo named Roo-roo. Roo-roo was unlike any other kangaroo in the country; He had boundless curiosity and an insatiable desire for adventure.

One sunny morning, while Roo-Roo was walking around the bush, he noticed something shimmering in the distance. With her large, expressive eyes, she gazed at it in awe. It was the sparkling blue water of a pristine lake he had never seen before. Ru-ru's heart was filled with excitement, and she decided that it would be a perfect day for an adventure.

Approaching the lake, Ru-ru saw a small boat tied to a tree. It was just his size! He knew what he had to do. He climbed into the boat, untied the rope, and with a mighty push, set sail into the crystal-clear water. As Roo-Roo rowed further into the lake, he encountered all kinds of wildlife. Colorful birds chirped from the trees, fish leapt from the water, and butterflies danced in the warm breeze. Ru-ru couldn't help but smile as she realized how beautiful and diverse her homeland was. As he rowed along, he spotted a group of friendly frogs sitting on a lily pad. They shouted "Ribbit, ribbit!" Roo-Roo laughed and joined in, making new friends in no time.

Ru-ru continued his journey, and the lake seemed to stretch on forever. As he began to feel a bit tired, he saw something extraordinary - a waterfall cascading down from the mountain above. The water sparkled in the sunlight, and Ru-Ru knew she had to see it up close.

I ran towards the Ru-Ru waterfall with great determination. As he approached, a mist of falling water spread over his fur, chilling him. It was refreshing and invigorating. Ru-ru got out of the boat and climbed the rocks to reach the top of the waterfall. At the top, he finds a hidden cave behind cascading water. Inside, he discovered a treasure chest filled with shiny, colorful stones and gems. Ru-ru's eyes widened in surprise. He stumbled upon a secret treasure! Ru-ru knew she couldn't carry the heavy chest all the way home, so she decided to leave it there, making a mental note of where she found it. He was content to know that the treasure was waiting for him whenever he wanted to see it again.

With a heart full of joy and a head full of unforgettable memories, Ru-Ru returned to the shore, where his adventure began. The sun is setting, casting a warm, orange glow on the outside. Ru-ru felt grateful for the incredible day she had experienced.

When she returned home, Ru-ru couldn't wait to tell her family about her amazing adventure. He realized that adventure is not just about traveling to faraway places; It was also about discovering the beauty and wonder that could be found in his own backyard.

From that day on, Ru-Ru never stopped exploring and learning about the world around her. He knew that every day held the possibility of a new and exciting adventure, whether big or small.

And so, Roo-roo, the little kangaroo with boundless curiosity, continues to live her life to the fullest, teaching everyone that the most amazing adventures can be found in the simplest moments and the places closest to your heart.

the end

Billy's Big Bounce

Once upon a time, in a sunny corner of the Australian outback, lived a young kangaroo named Billy. Billy was a curious and energetic kangaroo, known for his incredible bouncing skills. He was the smallest kangaroo in his family, but he had the biggest heart and the bravest attitude.

One bright morning, as the sun painted the sky pink and orange, Billy awoke feeling unusually restless. He looked at his reflection in a nearby waterhole and thought, "I want to do something amazing today!"

Billy ran to his mother, Mama Roo, who was busy grooming his soft, brown fur. "Mama, I want to see what lies beyond our valley," he said with hope in his eyes.

Mama Roo smiled fondly at her little kangaroo. "Billy, the world outside is vast and full of wonders," he said.

"But it can also be dangerous. Promise me you'll be careful."

Billy nodded eagerly, "I promise, Mama!"

With Mama Roo's blessing, Billy begins his adventure. He hopped through the long grass and climbed over the rocks, feeling the warm breeze on his fur. He bounced through the eucalyptus forest, befriending colorful birds and curious lizards along the way.

As he got farther from the house, Billy noticed something in the distance—a huge mountain that seemed to touch the sky. His heart was pounding with excitement. "This is it! I want to jump to the top of that mountain," he thought to himself.

Billy begins his climb, leaping and bounding higher with each leap. He can feel the thrill of the adventure through his veins. Along the way, he encounters a wise old kangaroo named Kenny. Kenny saw many young kangaroos trying to climb like Billy.

"Hello, young man," Kenny greeted Billy with a warm smile. "Are you aiming to reach the top of this mountain?"

Billy nodded eagerly, "Yeah, I want to see what's up there!"

Kenny's eyes widened in realization. "Remember, Billy, it's not just about how high you can bounce. It's about being patient, persistent and believing in yourself."

With Kenny's advice in mind, Billy continued his climb. The hill was steeper than he imagined and the journey was full of challenges. There were slippery rocks, gusty winds, and even a rain shower soaking his fur. But Billy didn't give up.

With each bounce, he grew stronger and more determined. Along the way he met friendly animals who cheered him on and he made new friends. The journey becomes as important as the destination.

After what felt like an eternity, Billy finally reached the top of the hill. He looked out over the vast expanse of the outback, feeling a sense of accomplishment like never before. The view was breathtaking and Billy knew he had achieved something extraordinary.

Kenny appeared once more as he began his descent. "Well done, Billy," she said, her eyes welling up with pride. "You learn that the journey can be just as exciting as the destination."

Billy nodded, grateful for the valuable lesson he had learned. With renewed confidence, he returns to his family, excited to share his adventures with Mama Roo and his siblings.

From that day on, Billy continued to explore the outback, but he never forgot the importance of being patient, persistent, and believing in himself. And whenever he felt the need for a big bounce, he'd head back to the mountains, not just for the breathtaking views, but to relive the journey that made him the extraordinary kangaroo.

And so, the little kangaroo with a big heart and boundless spirit continued to inspire those who met him with his incredible bounces and even more incredible stories.

Kangaroo Kaitlyn and the Golden Leaf

Once upon a time in the vast Australian outback, there lived a curious and adventurous kangaroo named Kaitlyn. Kaitlyn was known for her striking brown fur and her boundless curiosity. She lived with her kangaroo family in a cozy burrow under the shade of a towering gum tree.

One sunny morning, as Kaitlyn hopped around with her friends, she overheard a whispered rumor about a magical golden leaf. It was said that this leaf had the power to grant a single wish to the one who found it. Kaitlyn's big, brown eyes sparkled with excitement. She knew she had to find this golden leaf and make a wish.

Without wasting a moment, Kaitlyn bid her family and friends farewell, promising to return with the golden leaf. With her heart filled with determination, she began her journey into the vast and mysterious outback.

Days turned into weeks as Kaitlyn hopped across the scorching desert, through thick eucalyptus forests, and over rugged hills. She faced many challenges, like avoiding cunning dingoes and leaping over prickly bushes. Yet, Kaitlyn's determination never wavered.

One evening, as the sun painted the sky with shades of orange and pink, Kaitlyn came across a wise old kangaroo named Walter. Walter had traveled far and wide and knew the outback like the back of his paw.

Kaitlyn shared her quest with Walter, and he offered to help her find the golden leaf. "But," he said, "you must promise to use your wish wisely."

Kaitlyn agreed, and the two kangaroos set out together, following Walter's guidance.

They hopped through the night, and at the break of dawn, they arrived at a shimmering oasis.

In the heart of the oasis stood a magnificent golden tree, its leaves glistening in the sunlight. Kaitlyn's eyes widened with awe. She knew that the golden leaf she sought must be on that tree.

Kaitlyn and Walter approached the tree, and there, hanging from a branch, was the most beautiful golden leaf they had ever seen. Kaitlyn carefully plucked it from the tree, her heart racing with anticipation. As Kaitlyn held the golden leaf in her paw, she thought long and hard about her one wish. She could wish for anything, but what was the most important thing in the world to her?

Then, she realized it. Her wish was to bring back fresh water to her parched homeland, where the drought had caused so much suffering. With a deep breath, Kaitlyn closed her eyes and made her wish. She could feel the golden leaf glow in her paw, and then, a miracle happened. The once-dry land around the oasis began to flourish. Streams of crystal-clear water gushed forth, filling the riverbeds and quenching the thirst of all the animals in the outback.

Kaitlyn's heart swelled with happiness as she watched her wish come true. She had used her one wish to bring life and hope to her homeland, and that was the greatest gift of all.

With a grateful heart, Kaitlyn said goodbye to Walter and hopped back to her family and friends, who welcomed her with open arms. She shared her incredible journey and the importance of using wishes wisely.

From that day forward, the golden leaf remained a symbol of hope and kindness in the outback, reminding all who heard the tale of Kangaroo Kaitlyn and the Golden Leaf that the truest magic lies in helping others.

Hoppy and His Secret Hideout

Once upon a time in the sunny outback of Australia, there lived a young kangaroo named

Hopi. Hopi was known far and wide for his incredible jumping ability. His friends often gathered to watch him run higher and farther than any other kangaroo on land. But Hoppy had a secret and was excited to share it with his friends.

On a warm and breezy afternoon, Hoppy gathered his closest friends - Ruby the wallaby,

Benny the emu and Joey the koala. They sat in the shade of a tall gum tree, their eyes wide with curiosity as Hopi laughed mischievously. "Hey, everyone," Hoppy began, "I've got a secret to show you, but you don't have to tell anyone!"

His friends exchanged excited glances and nodded eagerly, promising to keep the secret.

With that, the Hopi led them deeper into the outback, scrambling over rocks and streams, until they reached a massive rock formation that looked like a wall. He approached it and whispered, "Look!" With a mighty leap, Hoppy soared higher and higher through the air, until he disappeared behind the rocky wall. Ruby, Benny and Zoey gasped in surprise. It seemed like he disappeared into the air!

Moments later, Hopi's head rested on the rock and he motioned for them to follow. They jumped with all their might, as had the Hopi, and soon they too were on the other side.

To their surprise, they found themselves in a secret paradise. It was a green oasis filled with colorful flowers and bubbling streams. Tall trees provided cool shade and the scent of eucalyptus leaves filled the air. "This is my hideout," Hoppy announced proudly. "I came here to rest and escape from the world. This is my special place, and now it's ours too."

The friends spent their days exploring the hidden paradise. They played games, talked, and even had picnics under the shade of a gum tree. Benny, the emu, showed off his running skills, while Joey, the koala, climbed trees with ease. Ruby, the wallaby, wanders around, joining Hoppy in a friendly jumping contest.

One day, while they were enjoying their hideout, they noticed a group of kangaroos from a nearby colony. The Hopi recognized them as his distant relatives. He was worried that they would reveal the location of the secret out.

"What do we do?" Ruby asked worriedly.

Hoppy thought for a moment then got an idea. He invited his relatives to join in the fun without revealing his secret hiding place.

They agreed and had a blast, not suspecting anything unusual.

Time passed, and Hopi's hideout became a place of joy and laughter for all his friends and relatives. They respected privacy and kept it hidden from the world.

As the years go by, Hoppy and his friends continue to cherish their special hideout, share countless adventures, and create wonderful memories together. It teaches them trust, the value of friendship and the importance of keeping promises.

And so, the hidden oasis remains a secret, known only to those who believe in the magic of friendship, loyalty and the incredible power of kangaroo jumping.

Kangaroo Kyle's Camping Trip

Once upon a time in the vast and sunny outback of Australia, there lived a young kangaroo named

Kyle. Kyle was known throughout the kangaroo community for his boundless energy and his insatiable curiosity. He was always looking for new adventures, and today was no different.

One bright morning, Kyle woke up with a twinkle in his eye. He heard about something exciting from his kangaroo friends: camping! He didn't know what it was, but it seemed like a great adventure. So, he went to his best friend, Caitlin's house.

"Caitlin, have you ever been camping?" Kyle asked, his eyes sparkling with excitement.

Caitlin, an intelligent kangaroo with a knack for outdoor adventures, nodded. "Yes, Kyle, I've been camping before. When you go out into the desert and spend the night in a cozy tent under the stars. It's so much fun!"

Kyle's heart leapt with joy. "I want to go camping too! Will you take me, Caitlin?"

Caitlin couldn't resist Kyle's enthusiasm. "Sure, Kyle! We'll plan a camping trip together."

They gathered their camping gear: a sturdy tent, sleeping bag, flashlight and some tasty food. Caitlin taught Kyle how to set up a tent and soon, they had a cozy little campsite ready.

As the sun began to set, they marveled at the beauty of the outback. The sky was painted orange and pink and the stars began to twinkle. Kyle had never seen anything so magical.

"Wow, Caitlin, that's amazing!" Kyle exclaimed as they sat by the campfire roasting marshmallows.

Caitlin smiled. "It sure is, Kyle. Camping allows us to connect with nature and enjoy life's simple pleasures."

They told campfire stories, and Kyle was mesmerized by Caitlin's tales of outback adventures. Imagining himself as a brave adventurer, he listened intently.

As night fell, they crawled into their sleeping bags inside the tent. Kyle stared up at the starry sky through the mesh roof of the tent. "Caitlin, do you think there's a kangaroo constellation out there?"

Caitlin laughed. "Well, why don't we make one? See three bright stars in a row? It could be 'Kyle's Tail'!"

Kyle laughed, "And those two stars could be 'Caitlin's ears'!"

They laughed together, forming their own kangaroo constellation.

A light rain started in the middle of the night. Kyle and Caitlin snuggled deeper into their sleeping bags, listening to the soothing patter of raindrops on the tent.

Morning is the song of birds. Kyle and Caitlin emerge from the tent, feeling refreshed and energized.

"We should do this more often, Caitlin," Kyle said, stretching out his long legs.

Caitlin nodded. "Of course, Kyle. Camping is a great way to appreciate the beauty of our home."

They pack up their campsite, leaving no trace behind, and return to their kangaroo community.

Kyle's camping trip was a great adventure and he couldn't wait to share his stories with his friends.

From that day on, Kangaroo Kyle became known as the adventurous kangaroo who went camping.

He cherished the memory of that starry night and looked forward to more camping trips with Caitlin in the future.

And so, in the heart of the Australian outback, Kyle the Kangaroo learned that adventures could be found right in his own backyard, and that the magic of camping would forever be part of his boundless curiosity and love of the great outdoors.

Ruby Roo's Rainbow Quest

Once upon a time in the heart of the Australian outback, lived a curious young kangaroo named Ruby Roo. Ruby was known far and wide for her vibrant red fur, which shimmered like the setting sun. But Ruby had a dream that set her apart from the other kangaroos. He wanted to find the legendary Rainbow Valley, a place that was supposed to hold the world's most beautiful rainbow.
One sunny morning, Ruby emerged from her cozy hole, determined to make her dream come true. He packed a small bag with some eucalyptus leaves and a water bottle, as he knew the journey would be long. As he embarks on his adventure, his kangaroo friends gather around to wish him luck.
"Watch out, Ruby Roo!" called his friend Joey. "The outback can be a tricky place."
Ruby nodded and left with a smile. His journey began.
For days, Ruby walked across the vast, red desert, with only the bright sun during the day and twinkling stars at night. He met friendly emus and wise old wallabies who shared stories of their own adventures. He listened attentively to their suggestions, which would be very helpful.
One evening, as the sun sank below the horizon, Ruby came across a sparkling oasis. The water reflects the colors of the sky, creating a beautiful, natural rainbow. Excitement filled his heart as he thought he had found Rainbow Valley. But the wise old wallaby, Wally, who lived nearby, told her, "It's a beautiful oasis, Ruby, but the real Rainbow Valley is still ahead. Go on, dear."

Ruby continued her journey with renewed determination. He galloped through green forests and crossed bubbling streams, always keeping an eye on the elusive rainbow. He met a wise old pregnant woman named Wilma, who shared stories of courage and perseverance. Ruby felt encouraged to move on.

As Ruby ventured deeper into the outback, the days grew hotter, and the journey more challenging. He encountered a tricky river with a strong current. As Wilma's words echoed in his mind, he carefully jumped from rock to rock, never losing sight of his aim.

One morning, after many weeks of travel, Ruby reached the highest peak in the Outback.

Before his eyes, the sky transformed into a magnificent rainbow, more vivid and beautiful than he had imagined. Ruby Ru's heart trembled with joy. He found Rainbow Valley!

But as he approached, something magical happened. The rainbow seemed alive, and from its colorful arches, a gentle, friendly rainbow kangaroo appeared. "Greetings, Ruby Roo," said Rainbow Kangaroo. "I am Roy the Rainbow Kangaroo, guardian of Rainbow Valley."

Ruby was surprised. He introduced himself and told Roy about his quest. Roy smiled warmly, "You've shown a lot of determination and kindness on your journey, Ruby. As a reward, you can visit Rainbow Valley whenever you like."

Ruby Ruby was delighted. She spent her days exploring the Vibrant Valley, befriending other rainbow-colored creatures, and dancing under the ever-bright rainbow.

With her heart full of joy, Ruby Ru knew her journey was worth every hop. He realized that sometimes, the most beautiful things are not found at the end of the rainbow but within the journey itself, filled with courage, perseverance and the kindness of friends along the way.

And so, Ruby Roo returns home, sharing her incredible rainbow quest with her kangaroo friends, who were inspired by her adventures. Ruby's vibrant red fur is now brighter, a reminder that dreams, no matter how colorful, can come true with determination and a bit of magic.

Kipper's Kangaroo Art

Once upon a time, in a small and colorful town, there lived a young kangaroo named Keeper. Keeper was known throughout the city for his boundless curiosity and love of art. He set up a small studio in his backyard, where he spent hours creating beautiful paintings.

One sunny morning, Keeper wakes up with an idea that fills his heart with excitement. He decided that he wanted to create a masterpiece that would amaze everyone in the city. When he stepped out of his comfortable pouch, he knew what his masterpiece would be - a painting of the stunning landscapes surrounding their city.

Keeper gathered his paintbrushes, colored paints and a canvas as big as himself. He embarks on an adventure to explore the natural beauty of the land. The grass was green, the sky was blue, and the flowers were in full bloom. The keeper couldn't be happier. He rushes from place to place, taking in every detail.

As he sits by the river, he sees a family of swans gliding over the water. Their reflections sparkle in the sunlight, creating a magical scene. Kiper dipped his brush in paint and began recreating this beautiful scene on his canvas. His strokes were gentle, and his color vivid. It was a perfect start.

Next, the keeper entered the forest. Tall trees surrounded him, leaves rustling in the wind. He saw a wise old owl sitting on a branch, watching over the forest. The keeper couldn't resist drawing the owl with its big, round eyes and feathery wings. The forest comes alive on his canvas.

As he continues his journey, he climbs a small hill and is greeted by the most magnificent view of the city. The houses, each with their unique colors, formed a beautiful mosaic. Kiper captured this scene, making sure to include every little detail.

The hours turned into days, and the keeper worked tirelessly on his masterpiece. He painted rolling hills, flowing rivers, bustling cities and even the bright sun. Each stroke of her brush filled the canvas with the love and wonder she felt for her home.

Finally, after days of hard work, the keeper stepped back and admired his creation. It was truly a masterpiece - a stunning depiction of the city's natural beauty. The keeper felt a sense of pride and accomplishment like never before.

He decided to share his masterpiece with the whole town. He invited everyone to the town square for an art exhibition. As the townspeople gathered around, their jaws dropped in amazement. They could not believe their eyes. Kipper's painting was a work of art that captured the essence of their city.

The mayor, who was an art enthusiast, was so impressed that he declared the keeper's painting the official city symbol. Keeper's artwork was framed and displayed in the town hall for all to see and admire.

Keeper's kangaroo art became famous far and wide. People came from nearby towns to visit and see the incredible paintings. Kiper's dream of creating a masterpiece had come true, and he was ecstatic.

Since that day, Kipper has continued to create beautiful artworks that celebrate the beauty of their city. He realized that art has the power to bring people together and fill their hearts with happiness.

And so, Keeper the Kangaroo, with his boundless curiosity and love of art, lived happily ever after sharing the beauty of their city through his incredible paintings. His story becomes an inspiration to All, reminding them that with passion and dedication anyone can create something truly amazing.

the end

Mia and the Mysterious Kangaroo Dance

Once upon a time in a far away country lived a curious girl named Mia. He was known in his small village for his insatiable curiosity and his boundless love for animals. Mia had a special place in her heart for kangaroos.

He has seen pictures and read stories about them in books, but he has never seen them in real life. His dream was to meet a kangaroo and learn about their unique ways.

One sunny morning, Mia's mother called her from the kitchen. "Mia, do you want to come to the market with me today?" she asked.

Mia's eyes lit up with excitement. "Sure, Mom! I'll be ready in a minute!" Mia loved going to the market with her mother. It was always an adventure, and he would often find little surprises like colorful rocks, beautiful seashells, or unusual fruits.

As they walked through the market, Mia's eyes wandered from vendor to vendor. Suddenly, something extraordinary caught his eye - a poster that read: "Mysterious Kangaroo Dance Tonight in the Village Square."

"Mia, look!" He pointed to the poster and said. "There's going to be a kangaroo dance tonight!"

Her mother smiled. "That sounds like fun, Mia. We should go."

Mia's heart skipped a beat as she imagined what the kangaroo dance would be like. He could hardly wait for the evening.

As the sun set, Mia and her mother walked into the village square. The place was buzzing with villagers who had gathered to witness the mysterious kangaroo dance. There was an air of anticipation as the villagers chatted about what they thought would happen.

Finally, the moment has arrived. The village elder, Mr. Jenkins, stepped onto a small platform. "Ladies and gentlemen," he announced, "tonight, we have a special treat for you all - a mystical kangaroo dance!"

Mia's heart skipped a beat in excitement. He couldn't believe that he was about to witness something so amazing.

Suddenly, the stage curtain opened, revealing a group of dancers dressed as kangaroos. They had kangaroo masks, furry tails, and walked like real kangaroos. The villagers clapped their hands and cheered.

But Mia noticed something unusual. One dancer stood out from the rest. He had a real kangaroo pouch, and his eyes twinkled mischievously. Mia was sure that this was a real kangaroo in disguise!

Unable to control her curiosity, Mia turned away from her mother and approached the mysterious kangaroo dancer.

"Hello there," Mia whispered. "Are you a real kangaroo?"

The kangaroo dancer nodded with a wink, and with a graceful leap led Mia to a secluded spot.

"I'm the kangaroo Kira," she said in a soft voice. "I wanted to dance with the villagers and show them how kangaroos move."

Mia's eyes widened in surprise. "You're amazing! But why keep it a secret?"

Kira smiled. "Kangaroos are usually shy around people, and I wanted to shock everyone. But you, Mia, have a good heart, and I knew you'd understand."

Mia was thrilled to make a new friend, especially a kangaroo! He watched in awe as Kira whooped and danced with the other performers.

The mysterious kangaroo dance turns into an unforgettable night for the villagers, thanks to Mia's new friend the kangaroo Kira. And Mia, with a heart full of joy, learns that sometimes dreams come true in the most unexpected ways. From that day on, he knew the world was full of wonderful wonders, just waiting to be discovered.

Kangaroo Kristy's Space Adventure

Once upon a time in the vast outback of Australia, there lived a young
kangaroo named Christy. He was a curious and adventurous kangaroo,
always seeking excitement outside the confines of his family's
comfortable confines.

One bright morning, as the sun painted the sky orange and pink,
Christy awoke with an idea that made her heart skip a beat. He heard
stories of the night sky, the stars and the moon from his elders. Christy
wondered what they would look like up close. He imagined himself
leaping among the stars and dancing with the moon.

"Today," he thought, "I'm going to have my own space expedition!"
Christy wasted no time. He got out of his cage and ran to his best
friend Joey. "Joey, I have a great idea!" he exclaimed.

Joy blinked sleepily. "What do you think, Christy?"

"I want to go to space and see the stars and the moon up close!"
Christy wondered.

Joy's eyes widened in surprise. "Space? It's incredible! But how do you
get there?"

Christy thought for a moment. "I've heard of a special place called the
'Outback Space Center'. Not too far from here. Let's go there and ask
if they can take us into space!"

Joey agrees, and the two friends begin their journey. On the way, they
met koala Kate, who was munching on eucalyptus leaves.

"Where are you going, Christy and Joey?" she asked.

Christy replied excitedly, "We're going to the Outback Space Center
for a space mission!"

Koala Kate smiled, "That sounds like quite an adventure! Follow me; I'll show you the way."

With Kate's guidance, they arrive at the Outback Space Center. It was a huge, silver building with a rocketshaped entrance. Christy and Joey sneak in and meet Eddie, a friendly emu who works at the center.

Eddie smiled kindly at their request. "We don't have rockets that can take you into space, but we do have something special." He led them to a large telescope.

"This telescope can bring the stars and the moon closer to you," Eddy explained.

Christy and Joey were thrilled. They wandered through the telescope and were mesmerized by the twinkling stars and soft glow of the moon.

As they gaze up at the night sky, Eddie shares stories about the constellations, the planets, and the wonders of the universe. Christy and Joey learn about the Milky Way and the different phases of the moon. They were so engrossed in the story that they lost track of time.

Finally it was time to go home. Christy and Joey thank Eddie and Koala Kate for their help and return to their burrow. When they returned, they looked up at the night sky, feeling a deep sense of wonder and happiness.

The next day, Christy and Joey couldn't stop talking about their space expedition. They realized that even without physically traveling in space, they learned a lot about the universe and felt a special connection with the stars and the moon.

From that day on, Christy and Joey spent many nights together gazing at the stars, sharing stories and imagining their own adventures among the stars. And while they never ran into space, they knew the wonders of the universe were always a telescope away.

And so, Kangaroo Christy's space adventure became a cherished memory, reminding them that curiosity and imagination can take them on incredible journeys, even without land.

Bouncing Benny's Birthday Surprise

Once upon a time in a cozy kangaroo family, there was a young and energetic kangaroo named Benny. Benny was known far and wide for his incredible bouncing skills. He could jump much higher and farther than any other kangaroo in the outback.

One sunny day, when Benny is walking through the green eucalyptus forest with his best friend Ruby the Rabbit, he can't contain his excitement. "Ruby, guess what?" Benny said, his eyes twinkling with excitement.

"What is it, Benny?" Ruby asked, her long ears perking up.

"Well," began Benny, "tomorrow is my birthday!"

Ruby's brows trembled with joy. "That's fantastic news, Benny! How old are you?"

Benny thought for a moment. "I'm going to be six, Ruby, and I want to do something special for my birthday."

Ruby smiled. "What are you thinking?"

Benny jumped up and down in excitement. "I want to have the biggest and most amazing bouncing contest ever! I want all my friends to join, and the winner will get a surprise prize."

Ruby nodded enthusiastically. "That sounds like a great idea, Benny!"

Benny spent the rest of the day inviting his friends to a bouncing contest. Kangaroos, wallabies and even some emus and koalas decided to join the fun. Everyone is thrilled with Benny's birthday surprise.

The next morning, the sun painted the sky with warm colors as Benny gathered with his friends in a large clearing in the outback. The bouncing competition is about to begin. Benny was the first to bounce and he went higher than ever. The crowd cheered, amazed at his skill. One by one, Benny's friends try to outdo each other. There was laughter and joy as they jumped and bounced, and everyone was having a great time. Even Ruby the Rabbit tried it out, and even though she didn't jump much, she definitely gave it her all.

As the competition continues, the judges notice a small wallaby named Wally. He was not jumping as high as Benny, but had a unique way of spinning in the air, which impressed everyone with his grace and style.

After everyone's turn is over, it's time to announce the winner. The judges honored, and then they called out, "The winner of Bouncing Benny's birthday surprise contest is... Wally the Wallaby!"

The crowd erupted in cheers and applause as Wally stepped forward to receive his award, a beautiful gold medal. Benny was thrilled for his friend and realized that sometimes, it's not just about who can jump the highest but also about celebrating each person's unique talents. The day continues with games, delicious eucalyptus leaf cake and lots of fun. Benny couldn't have asked for a better birthday. She learned that sharing her special day with friends and celebrating their talents was the greatest surprise.

As the sun set on Benny's special day, he bounced around one last time, feeling grateful for the love and friendship that surrounded him. It was a birthday he would never forget, full of joy, laughter and the spirit of leaping away from the heights, just as a kangaroo should. And so, with bouncing hearts, the kangaroos walked through the outback, knowing that the love of friends was the greatest gift.

Roxy Roo's Treasure Hunt

Once upon a time, in the vast outback of Australia, there lived a young kangaroo named Roxy Roo. Roxy was known across the country for her boundless curiosity and adventurous spirit. One sunny morning, Roxy is wandering around the outback with her friends, stumbling upon an old, weathered map half buried in the red desert sand.

Excitement welled up in Roxy as she carefully picked up the map. It had markings that read an "X" and the word "Treasure" next to it. Roxy could barely contain her excitement. He knew this was the start of a great adventure.

Gathering her friends, a diverse group of animals including Joey the koala, Lily the kangaroo and Timmy the emu, Roxy showed them the map. Their eyes widened in surprise. Together, they decide to embark on a treasure hunt.

Following the clues on the map, they traveled through the vast outback. Along the way they have faced various adversities. They had to jump over rocky terrain, cross a crocodileinfested river and even outrun a group of mischievous dingoes. But Roxy and her friends face every challenge with courage and teamwork, and their bond grows stronger with each passing day.

As they follow the map, they discover clues hidden in nature—the shape of a gum tree, the pattern of kangaroo tracks, and the color of a sunset. Each clue brings them closer to the treasure and their hearts race in anticipation.

One evening, as the sun sank below the horizon, they reached the final clue: the entrance to a cave. The map led them to a secluded cave deep in the desert. With wary excitement,

they enter the dark, mysterious cave, their paws and feathers jingling with anticipation.

Inside, they found a shiny chest adorned with precious gemstones. Roxy opened it carefully, revealing a treasure trove of books, toys and treats. It was a treasure beyond their wildest dreams, but it wasn't gold or gems—it was knowledge and the joy of friendship.

The animals cheered and celebrated their discovery. They realized that the real treasure was the adventure they shared and the knowledge they gained along the way. Roxy knew it was a journey they would cherish forever.

With their hearts full of joy, Roxy and her friends return to their home in the Outback, bringing with them a wealth of knowledge and friendship. They shared their stories with all the animals they met, inspiring others to embark on their adventures and find the treasures found in the world around them.

From that day on, Roxie Roo was known not only for her curiosity and adventurous spirit, but also for her wisdom and kindness. He learned that true treasures are not always what they seem and that the greatest adventures are shared with friends.

And so, in the heart of the Australian outback, Roxie Roo and her friends continued to hop, play and explore, knowing that every day was a new adventure waiting to unfold.

the end

Kangaroo Kara's Cooking Chaos

Once upon a time, in a sunny corner of the Australian outback, lived a young kangaroo named Kara. Kara was known across the country for her boundless energy and curiosity. But there was one thing she wanted to do more than anything else – she wanted to learn how to cook.

Kara watched her mother prepare delicious meals for their kangaroo family. She watched her father make eucalyptus leaf stew and her older brother Kenny even tried her hand at baking gumdrop muffins. Kara, however, has never tried her hand in the kitchen. He decided it was time to change that.

One bright and sunny morning, while her family was out and about and playing, Kara decided to surprise them with homemade food. He gathered all the ingredients he could find: eucalyptus leaves, wild berries, and a handful of colorful flowers.

With determination on her face Kara began to examine. She mixed the leaves and berries together, added a splash of water and even threw in some flower petals for good measure. He stirred and mixed, tasting his spell along the way. But something wasn't right.

Kara's stew turned a rather unusual shade of green and had a strange taste that surprised her. He frowned, wondering what had gone wrong. Just then, his mother, Katie, and Kenny returned home, their noses twitching at the unusual smell that filled the air. "What's that smell?" Katie asked with a confused expression.

"I was trying to cook, Mom, but I think I messed it up," Kara casually admits.

Kenny, ever the supportive brother, took a small sip and exclaimed, "Well, that sure is unique, sister!"

Katie smiled, realizing that Kara had put a lot of effort into her cooking test. "Cooking takes practice, sweetheart," he said softly. "We all start somewhere. Let's try to fix it together."

Kara learned about proper ingredients and proportions under her mother's guidance. They added some fresh vegetables and herbs to the stew, making it taste even better. Kara's spirits soar as she begins to understand the art of cooking.

As they worked together, the stew's delicious aroma filled the air, attracting their neighbors – a group of friendly wallabies and koalas. They all join in eagerly, sharing stories and laughter.

Soon, Kara's stew was ready to serve. Everyone gathered around the makeshift picnic table made of logs, and Kara proudly served her first homemade meal. The stew, now a delightful shade of green, was a hit! The unique blend of flavors makes this a truly memorable dish.

Afterwards, Kara felt a warm sense of accomplishment as the sun began to set. She turned her cooking mess into a delicious success, and she realized that learning to cook wasn't just about making the perfect meal but about enjoying the process and sharing good times with loved ones.

From that day on, Kara continued to test and improve her cooking skills, creating new recipes that became beloved by their little community of kangaroos. She learned that cooking brought her family and friends closer, and she cherished the memories they made around the dinner table.

And so, in the heart of the Australian outback, Kangaroo Kara's Cooking Chaos becomes a delightful adventure of discovery and togetherness, proving that with determination and creativity, even the most chaotic beginnings can lead to the tastiest endings.

Jake and the Kangaroo Kingdom

Once upon a time, in a land far, far away, there lived a curious and adventurous boy named

Jake. Jack is like no other boy you've ever met; He had a heart full of courage and an insatiable thirst for exploration. Every weekend, he would embark on exciting journeys to the nearby forest, exploring new and magical places.

One sunny Saturday morning, Jack woke up extra early, full of excitement. He heard whispers from the townspeople about a place known as the "Kangaroo Kingdom". Legends had it that this kingdom was hidden deep in the forest and was inhabited by friendly kangaroos who could talk and perform incredible feats of acrobatics.

Determined to discover this wonderful place, Jack packs a small backpack with snacks, a water bottle and his trusty map. With his dog, Buddy, by his side, he headed into the thick woods.

As Jack and Buddy went deeper into the forest, they followed the clues on the map, which led them through twisting paths and under tall trees. The forest was alive with the chirping of birds and rustling of leaves, creating an enchanting atmosphere.

A few hours passed, and just as Jake was about to give up hope, he heard a soft rustling in the bushes. With a sigh, he approached and discovered a hidden passage. His excitement grew as he realized he was on the right track to the Kangaroo Kingdom.

The path led them to a clearing where an extraordinary sight awaited them. Kangaroos of all sizes gathered in the shade of giant eucalyptus trees. These kangaroos were unlike any Jack had ever seen; They wore colorful scarves and had mischievous glints in their eyes.

Carefully approaching the kangaroos, Jack introduced himself and Buddy. The kangaroos,

being remarkably friendly, came forward to greet them. One of the kangaroos, a wise old fellow named Roo-roo, stepped forward. Roo-roo told Jack about the Kangaroo Kingdom, a place where kangaroos lived in harmony with the forest and each other. They loved to put on daring acrobatic shows, leaping high into the air and doing graceful back flips.
Intrigued, Jack watched in awe as the kangaroos performed a dazzling display of acrobatics. He clapped and cheered with Buddy, who barked enthusiastically.

At the end of the show, Roo-Roo offers Jake and Buddy a trip to the Kangaroo Kingdom.

They explored verdant gardens filled with vibrant flowers and shimmering ponds where colorful birds fluttered around. It was a paradise of nature and wonder.
As the day turned to evening, Jake realized it was time to head home. He thanked Roo-roo and the other kangaroos for their hospitality, promising to return soon. With a wave goodbye, Jack and Buddy begin their journey through the forest.
The magical experience of Kangaroo Kingdom stayed with Jake forever. He often returns with his family, and together they marvel at the wonderful world of talking kangaroos. Jake learns that sometimes, the most amazing adventures are hidden in your own backyard, waiting to be discovered.
And so, the legend of Jack and the Kangaroo Kingdom became a beloved story in their town, inspiring other young adventurers to

follow their dreams and explore the wonders of the world around them.

Katie and the Kangaroo Carnival

Once upon a time, far away, in a colorful land, there lived a little kangaroo named Katie.

Katie was known for her boundless energy and curiosity. He always dreamed of something magical happening in his quiet little town. One sunny morning, while he was walking around the eucalyptus trees, he noticed a large, colorful poster next to one of the trees. It read, "Katie and the Kangaroo Carnival: Coming Soon!"

Katie's heart leapt with excitement. He couldn't wait to tell his friends about the carnival.

She gathered all her kangaroo friends, including Kevin, Kara and Cody, and shared the fantastic news. Kangaroo friends were thrilled and decided to make the carnival the best event ever!
Katie's first task was to find the perfect location for the carnival. With her firm, springy legs, she explored every nook and cranny of their town. After hours of jumping and searching, he discovered a beautiful meadow with green grass, surrounded by tall gum trees. It was the ideal venue for the carnival.
Next, Katie and her friends brainstorm ideas for carnival attractions. They decided to have a bouncy castle, a ferris wheel for kangaroos, a face painting booth and a delicious
eucalyptus leaf buffet. Katie was put in charge of the bouncy castle, while Kevin and Kara took care of the Ferris wheel and face painting, and Cody ran the buffet.

The days leading up to the carnival were filled with excitement and hard work. Katie and

her friends worked tirelessly together to set up the attraction. They decorated the bouncy castle with colorful streamers and balloons, painted a giant kangaroo face on the ferris wheel, and collected the yummiest eucalyptus leaves for the buffet.
Finally, the big day has arrived. The sun was shining brightly in the sky, and the meadow was humming with excitement. Kangaroos from all over the city came to Katie and the Kangaroo Carnival. There were baby kangaroos, old kangaroos, even kangaroos from neighboring towns!
Katie was at the entrance, welcoming all guests with her warm, friendly smile. As the kangaroos jumped around, they couldn't contain their joy. The bouncy castle was a huge hit, with the kangaroos jumping high in the air and laughing with glee. The Ferris wheel provides breathtaking views of the entire carnival, and the face painting booth turns kangaroos into colorful artwork.
But the highlight of the carnival was the eucalyptus leaf buffet. The kangaroos lined up to taste the delicious leaves that Katie and Cody had prepared. There were eucalyptus leaf salads, eucalyptus leaf smoothies and even eucalyptus leaf ice cream. The kangaroos couldn't get enough of the delicious food.
As the sun begins to set, Katie gathers all her friends and the town's kangaroos for a grand finale. They lit a bonfire, and the kangaroos danced around it, their hearts filled with joy. Katie's dream of a magical event came true and it was even more magical than she imagined.
Katie and the Kangaroo Carnival has become an annual tradition, bringing the kangaroo community together in happiness and harmony. Katie and her friends learn that when they work together

and put their hearts into something, they can create something truly extraordinary.

And so, by the glow of bonfires, with the stars twinkling above, the city's kangaroos celebrated their carnival, knowing that the magic of unity and friendship can make any dream come true.

Rusty's Kangaroo Rescue

Once upon a time, in the heart of the Australian outback, there lived a young man named Rusty. He was known for his adventurous spirit and his love for animals especially kangaroos. Rusty lived on a farm with his parents, who were wildlife conservationists.

One sunny morning, Rusty wakes up to the sound of an annoying kangaroo outside his window. He rushed outside to find a mother kangaroo huddled in a thornbush, with her little joey watching anxiously nearby. It seemed like they had been fighting for hours.

Without wasting a moment, Rusty grabbed his gloves and a pair of scissors and carefully approached the trapped kangaroo. He knew he needed to be gentle and calm. Slowly, he began to cut the thorny branches, being careful not to harm the kangaroo.

The mother kangaroo, sensing Rusty's kindness, was surprisingly calm. As soon as she was free, she took off, but her joey didn't follow. The baby kangaroo was too scared and confused to move.

Rusty gently picked up little Joey, holding him in his arms. He could see the worry in its eyes, and he knew he had to help reunite the child with its mother. He decided to name Joy "Ru" because it was the cutest name he could think of.

With Roo in his arms, Rusty follows Mother Kangaroo's tracks, from rock to rock and through the dry, dusty landscape of the outback. It was a challenging journey, and Rusty was determined to bring Roo back to her mother.

Finally they found the mother kangaroo resting in the shade of a gum tree. He was happy to see his son again. Rust gently placed Roo on her side, and the mother kangaroo nudged Joy with love and gratitude. Rust watched them for a while, feeling satisfied that he had reunited the kangaroo family. But his adventure was not over. On his way back home he noticed something in the distance. It was a group of kangaroos, including some young ones, who seemed to be in trouble. Without hesitation, Rusty approached the new group only to discover that they were trapped in a fenced area. The poor kangaroos had no way of escape, and looked frightened and exhausted.

Rusty knew he couldn't leave them there. He decided to call his parents for help. His parents rushed to the spot with tools and equipment to safely dismantle the fence. It took some time, but working as a team, they managed to free all the trapped kangaroos. Rusty felt a sense of accomplishment as the kangaroos bounded into the desert. He not only rescued Roo but also helped several other kangaroos find their freedom.

That evening, Rusty sat on his porch, tired but happy. He realized that even a young boy like him could make a big difference in helping animals. His love for kangaroos led him on an incredible adventure and he knew he would always be there to protect and rescue them whenever they needed him.

From that day on, Rusty's fame as a kangaroo hero spread throughout the outback and he became known as the boy who would go to great lengths to save his beloved kangaroos. And he continues to do just that, ensuring these iconic Australian animals can roam freely in their natural habitat.

Kangaroo Kyle's Kite Festival

Once upon a time, in a sunny and peaceful meadow, there lived a young kangaroo named Kyle. Kyle was known for his boundless energy and special love of flying things. He admired the birds that soared above him and dreamed of joining them in the sky.

One bright morning, as Kyle walks through the meadow, he stumbles upon a colorful poster. It read, "Meadowville Kite Festival - Join the Sky Adventure!" With excitement, Kyle knew this was his chance to be part of the sky.

Kyle rushes over to tell his mother kangaroo Karen about the festivities. "Mom, can I go to the kite festival and fly a kite?" he asked eagerly.

Karen smiled at the twinkle in Kyle's eye. "Of course, my dear. That sounds like a great idea. Let's make a kite together!"

They gathered materials - colored paper, thin bamboo sticks, and strong strings. Kyle's mom helped him make the most beautiful kite. It had rainbow colors and a long, flowing tail that flew like a ribbon.

The day of the Meadowville Kite Festival has arrived. Kyle clutched his kite tightly and ran to the festival grounds. There, he saw kites of all shapes and sizes: dragons, butterflies and even one that looked like a giant octopus! Kyle felt a mixture of excitement and nervousness in his stomach.

As the festival begins, everyone releases their kites into the sky. The air was filled with laughter and joy as kites danced in the air. Kyle hesitated but took a deep breath and let his kite fly into the sky. It fluttered and sweded, but it didn't soar like the others. Kyle tried again and again, but his kite wouldn't stay right.

His heart sank, and tears rolled down his eyes. Just then, a kind pelican named Polly notices her struggle. "Hey, little boy," Polly said with a warm smile. "Looks like you could use some help."

Polly showed Kyle how to adjust the string tension and angle the kite to catch the wind properly. Kyle listened intently and, with Polly's guidance, his kite finally soared high, joining the colorful chorus in the sky. Kyle's face lit up with joy as he watched his kite dance in the clouds.

As the day progresses, Kyle makes new friends, all eager to share their kite-flying tips. He learned from each of them and improved his skills. Kite festival has become a day full of laughter, fun and friendship. When the sun started to set, it was time to take down the kite. Kyle carefully lowered his kite and thanked Polly and his new friends for their help. With his kite safely away, he set off for home, his heart full of gratitude and joy.

That night, as Kyle slept in his cozy kangaroo pouch, he couldn't stop smiling. He realized that sometimes, even when things don't go perfectly, with a little help from friends, dreams can fly. He knew he would cherish this kite festival forever, and he couldn't wait for the next one.

And so, in the meadow, under the starry sky, Kyle the kangaroo drifted off to sleep, dreaming of soaring higher and higher with his kite in the endless blue sky.

Joey and the Moonlight Magic

Once upon a time, in the heart of the Australian outback, there lived a young kangaroo named Joey.

Joey was a curious and adventurous kangaroo who loved to explore the vast desert and jump across the red sand.

One warm evening, as the sun sank below the horizon, Joey noticed something remarkable. The full moon began to rise, and it shone like a giant pearl in the night sky. He had heard stories about the magic of the moon from his kangaroo friends, and tonight, he was determined to discover it for himself.

With a heart full of excitement, Joey set off into the desert. The night was cool, and the air was filled with the sweet scent of eucalyptus trees. Joey jumped along, guided by the soft glow of the moon.

As he ran far from his house, he noticed something strange. The red sand under his paws began to change color. It turned silver and sparkled like stardust. Joey couldn't believe his eyes; It was the magic of the moon at work.

Curiosity led him to explore this enchanted desert. Soon, he encountered a group of animals he had never seen before. They were tiny, bright creatures with wings. They danced and twinkled around him, casting a soft, charming light.

"Hello, little ones," Joey greeted them with a friendly smile.

"We are moon fairies," replied one of them. "We come out when the moon is full to cast her magic."

Jaya was mesmerized by the grace of fairies and the shimmering aura around them. They invite her to join them in their dance, and together they create a beautiful moonlight that paints the desert with brilliant colors.

As they danced and spun, the moonlight fairies shared stories of their adventures. They told Joey about the magical moonflowers that bloom only in the light of the full moon and how they helped animals in need with their moonlight magic.

Joey was curious and decided to ask for their help. He told them about his older kangaroo friend, Gramps, who was struggling to climb as high as he used to. Joey wished for the magic of moonlight to help Gramps regain his strength.

The moon fairies nodded and agreed to help. They took Joey to the moonlit field, which had begun to bloom just as they arrived. The fairies danced around Gramp, casting their magical moonlight upon him. Gradually, Joey saw a change in his dear friend. Gramps began to run further and faster than before, his eyes shining with new energy.

Joyful tears welled up in Joey's eyes as he hugged Gramps tightly. "Thank you, Moonlight Fairy! You bring magic into our lives."

The moonlight fairies smiled and continued their dance, spreading their enchantment across the desert. Joey knew he had made lifelong friends, and he promised to meet them when the moon was full.

From that day on, Joey and Gramps shared their moonlight magic with all the creatures of the outback. Whenever the moon was full, they would gather around the moon-faced flower, and the moon fairies would bless them with their magical dance.

Joey learned that true magic is not about spells or tricks but about the love and kindness we share with others. And in the heart of the Australian outback, under the twinkling light of a full moon, Joey and Gramps find the most extraordinary magic of all - the magic of friendship and helping those in need.

And so, the moon rose, pouring its silver glow outside, where Joey and his friends lived happily.

the end

Jumping Jax's Jungle Journey

Once upon a time, in a remote jungle, there lived a young and energetic kangaroo named Jumping Jacks. Jax was known throughout the jungle for his exceptional jumping skills. He could jump much higher than any other kangaroo and he loved to show off his impressive leaps to his friends.

One sunny morning, as Jax wandered around the woods, he heard a faint cry for help. It was coming from deep in the thick forest. Jax's long, pointed ears perked

up, and his heart raced in excitement. He ran towards the sound without thinking.

Navigating the dense foliage becomes more and more challenging as he ventures deeper into the forest. But Jax is determined to find the source of the tears. He jumped over fallen trees, skipped through streams, and scrambled through tangled vines, while faint cries for help followed.

Finally, after what felt like an eternity, Jax reached a clearing where he found a small, frightened monkey named Momo. Momo was stuck in a tall tree, with no way to get down. His hands and feet were shaking with fear.

"Help help!" Momo cried, seeing Jax. "I climbed up here to reach some delicious bananas, but now I can't get down!"

Jax's mind went to the little monkey in fear. He knew he had to do something. With a powerful leap, Jax reached the top of the tree where Momo was. He gently put the shivering monkey into his bag.

"Don't worry, Momo. I got you," Jax assured her with a warm smile. He then carefully climbed down from the tree, landing Momo safely on the ground with his pouch.

Momo hugged Jax tightly, tears of relief running down her hairy cheeks. "Thank you so much, Jumping Jax! You're my hero!"

Jax smiled, "No problem, Momo. I'm always here to help my friends." With that, he headed back to the edge of the forest, where he and Momo parted ways.

But Jax's adventure isn't over. As he continues his journey, word of his heroic rescue of Momo spreads throughout the forest. Creatures of all shapes and sizes began to gather around, seeking his help with various problems.

Jax was more than happy to help. He helped a lost toucan find its way home, rescued a baby sloth stuck in a tree, and even helped a group of chatty parrots find their lost friend. Jax realized that his incredible jumping ability could make a big difference in the jungle.

At the end of the day, Jax is exhausted but full of joy. He made many new friends, and the forest was a happier and safer place because of his efforts.

As the sun began to set, Jax retreated to his cozy den, feeling satisfied. He knew he might have more jungle adventures in the future, but for now, he was happy to help his friends when needed.

And so, the brave and kind hearted Jumping Jax walks through the jungle, always ready for his next jungle adventure and another chance to make a difference in the lives of his jungle friends.

Kangaroo Kat's Colorful Crayons

Once upon a time, in a sunny and lively land below, there lived a lively kangaroo named Cat. Kat was not like the other kangaroos around her. He had a special talent that set him apart - he could draw the most beautiful pictures using colored crayons.

Kat's pouch was always filled with an assortment of crayons of every color you could imagine. Red, blue, green, yellow, and even some colors you've probably never heard of like periwinkle and magenta. His pouch was like a treasure trove of creativity.

One sunny morning, Cat ran to her favorite spot under a gum tree, her pouch clinking to the sound of crayons. He was feeling particularly inspired that day. He looked up at the clear blue sky above him and thought, "I'm going to create a masterpiece today." Kat began to draw. With his steady paw, he painted a magnificent landscape. There were rolling hills, a sparkling river and towering eucalyptus trees. As she colored in the picture, the world around her came alive with vibrant colors.

Word quickly spread around the animal community about Cat's incredible talent.

Animals used to come from far and wide to see his works of art. They were amazed at his drawings and how the colors seemed to jump off the paper.

One day, Kat had a brilliant idea. He decided to organize an art show in his neighborhood. He wanted to share his love of art with everyone and inspire them to

be creative. So, he hung his colorful paintings around the gumtree where he lived.

The art show was a great success! Animals of all shapes and sizes admired Kat's artwork. They were also inspired to try their hand at painting. Some painted portraits of their families, some beautiful landscapes, and some created abstract masterpieces.

Cat's art show became an annual event, and each year, the artwork became more and more incredible. The land below was soon known for its artistic talent and artists from other countries came to see what all the fuss was about.

One day, a young koala named Kevin approached Kat with a problem. He lost his favorite crayon, a special shade of silver-grey, and he didn't know how to finish his masterpiece without it. Kat sees the sadness in Kevin's eyes and decides to help.

She emptied her crayon pouch and handed him her silver-grey pouch. "Here, Kevin," she said, "finish your drawing using my crayons. I'll manage with the other colors for a while."

Kevin was delighted by Kat's kindness. With silver-grey crayon, he completed his masterpiece, a stunning image of a silver moon over the Gumtree. It was beautiful and enchanting.

Kat's kindness spread across the country, inspiring everyone to share and help one another. The animals realized that the true magic of art was not just in color and form but that it brought them all together as a community.

And so, in the land below, Cat the Kangaroo continued to create her colorful crayon masterpieces, but the most beautiful masterpiece was the friendship and love that blossomed between the animals, thanks to Cat's colorful crayons and her even more colorful heart. .

Samantha's Secret Kangaroo Club

Once upon a time in a cozy little town called Kangarooville, there lived a spirited young woman named Samantha. Samantha had an insatiable love for kangaroos. Her room was decorated with kangaroo posters, stuffed kangaroos and even kangaroo-shaped pillows. He was known as Kangaroo Kid among his friends.

Samantha's biggest dream was to meet a real kangaroo. He longed to see them up close, run with them and even share a pouch with a baby kangaroo, called Joey. Every day after school, he

Went to the local zoo to see the kangaroos roaming around, but he yearned for something more.

One sunny afternoon, while Samantha was walking in Kangarooville Park, she saw a strange sign on a tree that read, "Kangaroo Lovers Only - Secret Kangaroo Club." His eyes widened in excitement. He followed a trail of painted kangaroo footprints and they led him deep into the forest of the park.

After walking for a while, Samantha stumbled upon a hidden clearing. In the middle of it was a magnificent kangaroo statue, and around it gathered other children who shared his love of kangaroos. They all wore red bandanas with kangaroo prints.

Samantha is welcomed by a friendly girl named Emily, the leader of the club. "Welcome to

Samantha's Secret Kangaroo Club! We are united by our love of kangaroos. We learn about them, protect their habitats, and sometimes, we even dress up as kangaroos ourselves!"

Samantha's mind danced with joy. He found his tribe! The kids taught him fascinating kangaroo facts. He learned that kangaroos are marsupials, meaning they carry their young in a pouch. They had powerful hind legs to leap great distances in a single bound.

The club also had a special mission. They collected donations to spread awareness about conserving kangaroo habitat and protecting these unique animals. Samantha felt proud to be a part of something so important.

On a sunny Saturday, the club hosted a kangaroo fun fair. There were kangaroo-themed games, a kangaroo costume contest and even a kangaroo-shaped cake! Samantha dressed as a kangaroo with a red bandana around her neck.

He couldn't help but smile as he wandered around the fairgrounds. Kangarooville was transformed into a kangaroo wonderland. Children and families from all over the city joined in the fun and learned about these amazing animals.

But the best surprise came at the end of the day. Kangarooville Zoo heard about the Kangaroo Fun Fair and decided to bring a real kangaroo to meet Samantha and her club members.

Samantha's heart raced with excitement as she came face to face with a real, live kangaroo named Ruby.

Ruby was polite and friendly. Samantha couldn't believe her luck. He fulfilled his dream of meeting a kangaroo, and it's all thanks to the club he joined.

From that day on, Samantha and her new friends continue to meet, learn about, and protect kangaroos. They even managed to convince the city to build a special kangaroo reserve where these magnificent animals can thrive.

Samantha's Secret Kangaroo Club has become a symbol of love, friendship and dedication.

Samantha not only made her dream a reality but also helped make the world a better place for kangaroos.

And so, in the heart of Kangarooville, a secret club with a secret mission jumps, skips and jumps towards a brighter future for their beloved kangaroos.

Kangaroo Ken's Kangaroo Caper

Once upon a time in the vast outback of Australia, there lived a young kangaroo named Ken.

Ken was unlike any other kangaroo in the crowd. A twinkle in his eye and a heart full of curiosity. While his kangaroo friends were content to graze on the grass, Ken dreamed of exciting adventures.
One sunny morning, Ken wakes up with an idea that fills him with excitement. He wanted to organize a kangaroo caper - an amazing race across the outback. He envisioned kangaroos of all sizes, running counter-clockwise through the red desert, leaping and bounding. Ken couldn't wait to share his idea with his friends.
"Hey everyone!" Why did he call the crowd? "I've got a great idea! Let's do a kangaroo caper race. It'll be so much fun!"
The other kangaroos looked at Ken with surprised expressions. They weren't sure what a kangaroo caper was, and they were quite comfortable with their slow, steady lifestyle.
"Why, are you sure of this?" asked her best friend Kylie. "We've never done anything like this before."

Ken smiled and replied, "That's the best part, Kylie! It's time to try something new and exciting!"

After much persuasion and prodding from Ken, the kangaroos agreed to give it a try. They start preparing for the big race. Ken's enthusiasm was contagious, and soon the whole crowd was excited about the kangaroo caper.

They marked a challenging course across the desert complete with hills, valleys and rocky obstacles. Ken was the race coordinator, and he worked tirelessly to make sure everything was perfect.

On Kangaroo Caper Day, kangaroos from all over gather to participate. Ken couldn't believe his eyes. There were kangaroos of all ages and sizes, eager to take part in the adventure.

The race begins with a loud cheer from the crowd. The kangaroos leaped and bounded with all their might. Ken, the fastest and most agile, was in the lead. But he didn't want to win; He wanted everyone to have a great time. So, he slowed down to run alongside his friends, encouraging them and giving them tips on how to overcome obstacles.

The race took them through burning deserts, cold streams and over huge rocks. It was hard, but it was incredibly fun. Kangaroos who had not experienced such excitement were full of a new zest for life.

As they neared the finish line, Ken saw a kangaroo named Tommy struggling up a steep hill. Without a second thought, Ken hopped back and extended a helping paw. Together, they conquer the mountain and reach the finish line.

The cheers and applause from the crowd were deafening as Ken and Tommy crossed the finish line together. It wasn't about winning; It was all about camaraderie and thrills.

After the race, Ken gathered his friends and said, "I hope you all had a great time today.

Remember, life is about trying new things and enjoying the ride together."

Since that day, the Kangaroo Caper has become an annual event in the Outback. Ken's dream came true, and the kangaroos now look forward to their exciting adventures every year.

And so, Kangaroo Kane's Kangaroo Caper taught everyone that sometimes, stepping out of your comfort zone and trying something new can lead to the most wonderful and unexpected adventures. And for Ken and his friends, every day in the Australian outback was an adventure waiting to happen.

Daisy's Daring Kangaroo Dive

Once upon a time, in the sunny and vast land of Australia, there lived a curious and adventurous little girl named Daisy. Daisy was known for her boundless energy and love for exploring the great outdoors. He lived near a beautiful forest and spent most of his days playing in the forest with his friends.

One sunny morning, while Daisy was swinging on her favorite tree swing, she heard a funny story from her friend Tommy. Tommy was on a camping trip with his family, and he told Daisy about a treasure deep in the woods. The treasure was said to be guarded by a magical kangaroo known to be the fastest and bravest kangaroo in Australia. Daisy's eyes sparkled with excitement as she heard Tommy's story. He decided that he would find this hidden treasure and meet the legendary kangaroo. She knew it was going to be a daring adventure, but Daisy loved a challenge.

The next day, Daisy packs a small backpack with water, snacks, and a map. He went into the forest following the path described by Tommy. The path was winding and covered in thick foliage, making it a challenging ride. But Daisy was determined, and she went on with unwavering enthusiasm.

As Daisy ventures deeper into the forest, she encounters a variety of wildlife and even sees a few kangaroos leaping between the trees. He wondered if one of them was the legendary kangaroo he had heard about. He decided to follow them, hoping they would lead him to the treasure.

A few hours passed, and Daisy felt tired, but her determination kept her going. Finally, he reaches a clearing where he sees a giant rock with strange markings. He consulted his map and realized that this was the place Tommy had mentioned.

Taking a breath, Daisy examined the rock closely. As he touched it, a hidden door in the ground opened, revealing a dark tunnel below. Without hesitation, Daisy descended into the tunnel, guided only by a glowing lantern she had brought.

Inside the tunnel, Daisy faced various challenges ranging from complex puzzles to crawling through narrow passages. He knew he was getting closer to the treasure, and his excitement grew with each step. Finally, at the end of the tunnel, he finds himself in a magnificent chamber filled with sparkling gems and gold coins.

But what caught his eye was a kangaroo statue made entirely of glittering gems. Daisy knew she had found the legendary treasure and the kangaroo statue was proof of that.

As he was about to collect his prize, a soft voice echoed in the chamber. It was the magical kangaroo, and it was not pleased with Daisy's presence. The kangaroo appeared before him, a majestic creature with shiny fur.

Daisy explained her quest and her desire to meet the brave kangaroo. The witch kangaroo listened and then nodded in understanding. It revealed that the treasure was not meant to be hoarded but shared with the world. The kangaroo also agreed to teach Daisy some daring tricks, such as jumping from high places.

Over the course of days, Daisy and the magical kangaroo become friends, practicing their daring dives and exploring the forest together.

Daisy learns valuable lessons about courage, friendship and the importance of sharing. And he had many daring adventures with his new found friend.

As the days turned into weeks, Daisy realized that the real treasure was not jewelry or gold but the incredible experiences and friendships she gained during her daring kangaroo dive.

And so, with a heart full of joy, Daisy said goodbye to the magical kangaroo and returned home, knowing that she had a daring adventure to remember and a friend who would always hold a special place in her heart.

Kangaroo Kody's Kangaroo Castle

Once upon a time, in the vast and vibrant Australian outback, there lived a young kangaroo named Cody. Cody was not like any other kangaroo; He was an adventurer at heart. He loved to explore new places and go on exciting journeys, but there was one dream he held closer to his heart than anything else: he dreamed of building a kangaroo fort.

One sunny morning, Cody gathered his kangaroo friends in the shade of a towering eucalyptus tree. "Listen, everyone," he said enthusiastically, "I have an idea. Let's build a kangaroo castle, a place where we can all play, laugh and have amazing adventures together!" His friends were thrilled at the idea. "That sounds amazing, Cody!" Ruby Roo turns out to be Cody's best friend. "But where should we build it?"

Cody thought for a moment and then pointed to a mountain in the distance. "How are you about?" she suggested. The hill had a perfect view of the surrounding outback and looked like the ideal location for a kangaroo fort.

The Kangaroos wasted no time. They gathered sticks, leaves and stones and rushed towards the hill. They worked tirelessly together, using their strong legs to dig holes for foundations and stack stones to form walls. Cody was the chief architect, guiding his friends with a vision in mind.

As they worked, they sang songs and shared stories about their adventures, which made the fort-building process more enjoyable.

Cody's friend, Joey, even found a shiny rock that they used as the magical center of the castle.

Days turned into weeks and Kangaroo Castle began to take shape. They added secret tunnels and hidden chambers and the castle started to look like a real castle. Cody couldn't be happier. His dreams were coming true, and he felt grateful for his amazing friends.

One day, as they were putting the finishing touches on Kangaroo Castle, they heard a soft cry nearby. They follow the sound and discover a lost baby kangaroo or a joey alone in the outback. Cody and his friends couldn't leave Joey alone. They decided to bring the little one back to Kangaroo Castle. They named him Sunny, and he quickly became a part of their close-knit kangaroo family.

With Sunny's arrival, Kangaroo Castle became more complete. They taught him how to jump and play games and Sunny's boundless energy brought endless smiles to the fort.

Cody's Kangaroo Castle has become a place of joy, friendship and adventure. Kangaroos from around the outback came to visit, and they shared their own stories and dreams. It wasn't just a castle; It was a symbol of unity and togetherness for all kangaroos.

And so, Kangaroo Cody's dream came true, not just for him, but for all the kangaroos of the Outback. They learn that dreams can be even more magical when you share them with friends and make the world a better place for everyone.

And so, Kangaroo Castle stands atop the hill, a testament to the power of dreams and friendship in the heart of the Australian outback, reminding everyone that adventure is best when shared with loved ones.

Zara's Zooming Kangaroo

Once upon a time, in a sunny land down under, there lived a little girl named Zara. Zara was known for her wild imagination and adventurous spirit. He loved exploring Australia's vast outback with his family. But what Zara loved the most was the kangaroo. He thought they were the most interesting animals in the world.
Every day, Zara went to the nearby bush to see the kangaroos. He marveled at their long, powerful legs and their incredible hopping ability. He imagined what it would be like to have a kangaroo friend.
One bright and sunny morning, as Zara watches a group of kangaroos from afar, she notices something unusual. Among the kangaroos was a baby kangaroo that looked different from the rest. It had attractive white fur and was smaller than the others.
Zara couldn't believe her eyes. He went back home to tell his parents about the special kangaroo he had seen. Her parents, seeing the excitement in her eyes, decide to investigate with her.
Together, they approached the bush, and to their surprise, they found the unique baby kangaroo alone. It seemed lost. Zara's heart went out to the little creature. He approached it gently and offered some water and food. The baby kangaroo, whom he decided to call Zoom, seemed to believe him.
Zara's family decided to take care of Zoom until they could find her mother or another kangaroo family to adopt. Zara was very happy to have a kangaroo as her friend. They become inseparable. Zoom would run around the backyard, and Zara would chase after him, giggling with delight.

But as the weeks passed, they realized that it would be difficult to find Zoom's real family. Zoom had a close bond with Zara and her family. They worry what will happen to Zoom if they find another kangaroo family for him.

One day, while Zara was playing with Zoom in the backyard, she had an idea. He remembered visiting a kangaroo sanctuary not far from their home. The sanctuary was a place where kangaroos that could not survive in the wild were cared for.

Zara and her family decide to go to the sanctuary and ask if they can provide a home for

Zoom. They explained the situation to the kind people who ran the sanctuary. They see love between Zara and Zoom and agree that Zoom will be safe and happy with them.

It was a bittersweet moment when Zara and her family brought Zoom into his new home. Zara knew it was the best thing for her special kangaroo friend. Zoom will have lots of other kangaroo friends to hop and play with.

As Zara bid farewell to Zoom, she felt a mixture of emotions. He was sad to say goodbye, but he also knew that he had given Zoom a chance to live his own happy life.

Zara's love for kangaroos never waned and she visited the sanctuary whenever she could.

And even though Zoom had a new family, he always remembered the little girl who was his first friend - the one who gave him the name Zoom.

Zara's heartwarming story of friendship with a kangaroo taught her that sometimes, doing what's best for the one you love means making a tough decision. And when he saw Zoom playing with his new kangaroo friends, he knew he'd made the right choice.

And so, Zara's adventures in the outback continued, the memory of Zoom forever etched in her heart.

Kangaroo Kate and the Kangaroo Choir

Once upon a time, in the vast and sunny outback of Australia, there lived a young kangaroo named Kate. Kate was a happy and curious kangaroo who loved to run around and explore her surroundings. He lived with his family in a cozy den under the shade of a eucalyptus tree. Kate was always fascinated by the sounds of nature. The chirping of birds, the rustle of leaves, the gentle breeze carrying the rustle of distant mountains—these filled his heart with wonder. But what intrigued him most was the rhythmic beat of his own kangaroo heartbeat and the soft, melodious hum of his family as they walked together.

One sunny morning, as Kate and her family were munching on some fresh eucalyptus leaves,

Kate had an idea. He decided to form a kangaroo choir! He believed that if they practiced together, their hopping and bounding could create a beautiful rhythm.
"Family, let's start a kangaroo choir!" Kate screamed in excitement. Her family members exchanged curious glances. They have never heard of such a thing. But seeing Kate's enthusiasm, they agree to try. Kate started by teaching them a simple hooping rhythm. They practiced every day, trying to do a count and stay in tune with each other. At first, it was a bit challenging. Kangaroos are known for their impressive leaps, but synchronizing those leaps with others was no easy feat.

Kate's family slowly improves as the days turn into weeks. Their hopping becomes more coherent, and the rhythm of their leaps begins to resemble a cheerful melody. They practiced in the early morning when the sun was just rising, filling the air with their newfound music.

One day, while the kangaroo choir was practicing, they heard a melodious chirp from a nearby tree. It was a little bird named Bella, who had been watching their rehearsal for days. Bella was so impressed with the kangaroo choir's efforts that she decided to join them. With her sweet singing voice, she added a beautiful melody to their whooping rhythm.

With Bella's contribution, the Kangaroo Choir's music becomes even more mesmerizing. News of their unique singing spread throughout the outback and the surrounding animals came to listen. Emus, koalas and even a wise old wombat gathered to enjoy the mesmerizing tunes of the kangaroo choir.

The Kangaroo Choir grew in popularity over time. They performed at special events and even in large gatherings of animals from near and far. The entire Outback was full of joy, thanks to Kate's ideas and her family's dedication.

But Kate knew that their real treasure was the unity and harmony they found as a family. Their music brought them closer than ever and it was the most beautiful melody.

One day, after a breathtaking performance, Kate and her family gathered under a eucalyptus tree. They smiled at each other, their hearts filled with gratitude and love.

"Kate, you had the most wonderful idea," said Kate's mother.

"We may have started a kangaroo choir, but it brought us closer as a family," added his father. Kate beamed with pride. "And it's the best music of all," he said.

And so, in the heart of the Australian outback, kangaroo Kate and her family continue to sing their unique tunes, bound in love and the joy of making music as a family.

Holly's Kangaroo Holiday

Once upon a time in a small town called Green Meadow, there lived a little girl named
Holly. Holly always dreamed of going on an exciting adventure. He had seen pictures and heard stories about kangaroos and their incredible jumping abilities and couldn't wait to see them up close.
One sunny morning, Holly's parents surprise her with the news that she is going on a special trip to Australia. Holly could not believe her ears! Australia was home to kangaroos, and it was going to be the adventure of a lifetime.
After a long flight, Holly and her family arrived in Australia. The moment they got off the plane, Holly's eyes lit up with excitement. The air was warm and filled with strange, pleasant scents.
Their first stop was a wildlife sanctuary where Holly would finally meet the kangaroos. As they entered the sanctuary, Holly saw a group of kangaroos in the distance. His heart raced in anticipation.
Holly approached them cautiously, her eyes wide in surprise. Kangaroos were big and strong, with long, strong legs. He watched as they leaped and bounded, effortlessly covering great distances in one leap.
Holly's parents encouraged her to move closer. He took a step, and then another, until he was standing a few feet from one of the kangaroos. He slowly held out his hand, and to his surprise, the kangaroo sniffed it curiously.

Holly giggled in delight as she gently stroked the kangaroo's soft fur. "Hello, Mr. Kangaroo," she smiled. The kangaroo seemed to enjoy the attention, and soon, more kangaroos came forward to greet him. Holly spent the rest of the day with the kangaroos. He learned that there are different types of kangaroo, each with its own characteristics. Some were tall, and others had dark fur. But they all had one thing in common - their incredible jumping ability.

As the sun began to set, Holly's family sat picnicking in the sanctuary. They shared stories and laughed together. Holly truly feels blessed to be surrounded by these amazing creatures.

The next day, Holly's family decides to explore more of Australia. They visited the Great Barrier Reef, where they saw colorful fish and swam with turtles. They explored the vast outback and saw kangaroos in their natural habitat.

Holly's kangaroo holiday was everything she hoped for and more. He made new furry friends, learned about Australia's unique wildlife and enjoyed the thrill of adventure.

As their journey ended, Holly felt a mixture of happiness and sadness. He knew he would miss the kangaroos and the beautiful Australian landscape. But he also knew he could always cherish the memories of his incredible kangaroo holiday.

With hearts full of gratitude, Holly and her family boarded the plane back to Green Meadow. As they flew home, Holly closed her eyes and dreamed of her kangaroo friends and all the amazing adventures that awaited her in the future.

And so, Holly's kangaroo vacation became a cherished memory, a reminder that sometimes the most extraordinary adventures can happen when you least expect them.

Kip and the Kangaroo Olympics

Once upon a time in the heart of the Australian outback lived a young kangaroo named Kip. Kip was known far and wide for his incredible jumping ability. His powerful legs can carry him high into the sky and he can run faster than anyone in the kangaroo community.

One sunny morning, while Kip was practicing his jumps and hops, his friend, Katie, a fellow kangaroo, ran up to him. "Kip," she said excitedly, "have you heard of the Kangaroo Olympics?"

Kip's ears perked up. "Kangaroo Olympics? Tell me more!"

Katie explains, "Kangaroo Olympics is a friendly competition between all the kangaroos in the

Outback. There are events like long jump, high jump and relay races. It's going to be a lot of fun!"

Kip's eyes sparkled with excitement. "I want to join the Kangaroo Olympics, Katie! Do you think I have a chance?"

Katie smiled. "With your amazing jumping skills, Kip, you have a better chance. You can win!"

Determined and excited, Kip began training hard. He practiced jumping over logs, leaping across rocky terrain and running against the wind. Katie was there every step of the way, cheering him on.

As the day of the Kangaroo Olympics approaches, Kip's excitement grows. He couldn't wait to compete against other talented Kangaroos and show what he's made of.

Finally, the big day has arrived. The Kangaroo Olympics were held in a large clearing surrounded by eucalyptus trees. Kangaroos gathered from all corners of the outback, each eager to demonstrate their unique skills.

The first event was the long jump. Kip took a deep breath and positioned himself at the starting line. With a mighty leap, he flew through the air, landing farther than the other kangaroos. The crowd erupted into cheers. Kip won the long jump event!

Then came the high jump. Kip faced a bar set higher than he had ever jumped before. He concentrated all his strength and jumped with all his might. Miraculously, he cleared the bar easily, setting a new Kangaroo Olympic record. The crowd cheered even louder.

Kip continues to dominate the competition as the day progresses. He won the relay race by racing with his friends, including Katie. Kip's team finished first, and they celebrated with joyful hops and bounces.

The Kangaroo Olympics ended with a grand ceremony. Kip stood at the podium, a gold medal around his neck, while Katie and her other friends proudly cheered him on. Kip felt a tremendous sense of accomplishment and gratitude.

But the best part of the Kangaroo Olympics wasn't the medals or records – it was the camaraderie and support of his fellow Kangaroos. Kip understood that the true spirit of the Olympics was to come together, have fun and encourage each other.

As the sun set over the outback, Kip and his friends returned home tired but happy. Kip knew the memory of the Kangaroo Olympics would stay with him forever.

And so, Kip the Kangaroo learns that with determination, hard work and the support of friends, he can achieve anything he sets his mind to. The Kangaroo Olympics not only made him a champion but also filled his heart with the joy of friendship and the thrill of competition.

It was a day he would cherish forever in the vast and beautiful Australian outback.

Kangaroo Krista's Kangaroo Kingdom

Once upon a time, in the heart of the Australian outback, there lived a
young kangaroo named
Krista. Krista was unlike any other kangaroo in her crowd. He had a
special dream - he wanted to create a kangaroo kingdom where
kangaroos of all shapes, sizes and colors could live in harmony.
Krista knew it wouldn't be easy, but she was determined to make her
dream come true. He started by talking to his friends and family about
his idea. At first they were skeptical. "Kangaroos always live in separate
crowds," they say. "Why change things?"
But Krista was persuasive, and slowly, one by one, she began to win
them over with her vision of a kangaroo kingdom. He explained that
they could all live together, help each other and share their stories and
experiences. After much talking and persuasion, her family and friends
agreed to give it a try.
Krista and her loyal friends began the hard work of building their
kangaroo kingdom. They cleared a vast area of the outback, ensuring
everyone had plenty of clean water and food. They built cozy dens and
nests where different populations of kangaroos could live side by side.
Kangaroo Kingdom was a diverse place, with kangaroos of all shapes
and sizes. There were big, strong kangaroos who were great at digging
holes, fast kangaroos who could scout for danger, and wise old
kangaroos who shared their knowledge of the land.
But it wasn't always smooth sailing. There were disagreements and
misunderstandings, just like in any community. Krista knew that in

order for the Kangaroo Kingdom to thrive, they had to learn to work together and respect each other's differences.

One sunny day, a group of kangaroos from another part of the outback arrived in the Kangaroo Kingdom. They were tired and hungry, having traveled a long way in search of a new home. Krista welcomes them with open arms and invites them to join the Kangaroo Kingdom.

At first, the newcomers were wary, but they soon found that Krista's kangaroo kingdom was a place of unity and friendship. They also started sharing their stories, skills and traditions. Gradually, the kangaroo kingdom became stronger and more vibrant.

In time, the news of the Kangaroo Kingdom spread far and wide. Kangaroos from all over the outback heard of a wonderful place where kangaroos of all backgrounds could coexist peacefully. They also wanted to be part of Christ's kangaroo kingdom.

And so, Kangaroo Kingdom continued to grow, becoming a shining example of unity and cooperation. Kangaroos of all kinds lived together, learning from each other and sharing their love for the beautiful outback they called home.

Krista's dream came true - she created a kangaroo kingdom where all kinds of kangaroos lived together in harmony. They played together, shared food and looked out for each other. It was a place where everyone felt welcome and valued.

Kangaroo Kingdom was not just a house; It was a family. Christa showed everyone that with a little patience, understanding and a lot of love, differences can be celebrated and unity can be achieved.

And so, in the heart of the Australian outback, Kangaroo Krista's Kangaroo Kingdom stood as a testament to the power of dreams and the beauty of diversity. It was a place where all kinds of kangaroos roamed together towards a brighter and more harmonious future.

And they all lived happily and peacefully.

the end

Bobby and the Kangaroo Cup

Once upon a time in the vast outback of Australia, there lived a young man named Bobby who was fascinated by kangaroos. Bobby had wild dreams about these amazing creatures and wanted to be bouncy like them.

One sunny morning, while Bobby was playing in his backyard, he saw a family of kangaroos walking by. He watched in awe as they galloped gracefully across the open field, their long tails trailing behind them.

Bobby knew he couldn't jump like a kangaroo, but he was determined to stay close to them. He decided to visit a local wildlife reserve, where kangaroos roamed freely. His parents agreed to take him.

At the reserve, Bobby saw kangaroos of all shapes and colors. Some were small and beautiful, others were tall and strong. There was even a kangaroo named Katie with a baby joey in her pouch. Bobby was thrilled to see them up close.

Bobby's favorite kangaroo was a friendly named Keeper. The keeper had soft brown fur and a gentle disposition. He lets Bobby feed on leaves and grass. They became fast friends, and Bobby would visit the keeper every weekend.

One day, while Bobby was feeding the keeper, he heard one of the zoo's kangaroos talking about a cup competition. It was a special event where kids from all over could participate in a kangaroo-themed challenge. The winner will receive the Kangaroo Cup.

Bobby's eyes lit up with excitement. He knew he had to compete. He rushed home and informed his parents. They supported and encouraged her to follow her dreams.

Bobby started training for the Kangaroo Cup. He practiced jumping around the backyard, trying to jump higher every day. He even started doing exercises to strengthen his legs. Bobby is determined to win.

The day of the Kangaroo Cup arrived, and Bobby was both nervous and excited. He saw all the children gathering at the reserve, each with their own stuffed kangaroo toy as a mascot. Bobby brought a small stuffed kangaroo he named "Hoppy".

The first challenge was a hopping race. Bobby lined up with the other kids, and when the race started, he gave it his all. As high and as far as he could, just like the keeper had taught him. And to his surprise, he did really well!

As the competition continues, Bobby faces more challenges like balancing on one leg like a kangaroo and imitating their hopping pattern. With each challenge, he became more confident. He felt like he was turning into a kangaroo himself.

Finally, it was time for the last challenge—a kangaroo-themed obstacle course. It was a test of speed, agility and jumping ability. Bobby knew that if he could conquer this course he might have a chance to win the Kangaroo Cup.

With determination and Hoppy by his side, Bobby tackles the obstacle course. He jumped over obstacles, darted through tunnels and balanced on narrow beams. It was a tough challenge, but Bobby gave it his all.

As Bobby crossed the finish line, the crowd erupted in cheers. He completed the course faster than anyone else! Bobby is awarded the Kangaroo Cup, and the keeper, his kangaroo friend, comes forward to congratulate him.

Bobby felt like he was on top of the world. He realized that even though he couldn't be a real kangaroo, he could be the best version of himself. He learned that with hard work, dedication and a little help from his kangaroo friends, he could achieve anything he set his mind to.

From that day on, Bobby continued to meet the keeper and other kangaroos in the reserve. He cherishes the memories of his Kangaroo Cup and his incredible adventures. And every time he looked at it, he was reminded that he could achieve his dreams, no matter how big they seemed.

Kangaroo Kim's Kangaroo Café

Once upon a time, in the heart of the Australian outback, there lived a friendly kangaroo named Kim. Kim was known far and wide for her boundless energy and her love of trying new things. But more than anything, Kim loved to cook delicious food.

One sunny morning, as Kim was walking through the eucalyptus forest, he had a brilliant idea. He wanted to open a cafe! But not just any cafe—a kangaroo cafe! He believed that everyone should taste the amazing flavors of the outback.

Kim immediately set to work, gathering leaves, berries and herbs to create unique recipes. He used his strong tail to mix and stir, and his pouch to carry his ingredients. He worked tirelessly to perfect his dishes.

Word of Kangaroo Kim's Kangaroo Cafe quickly spread through the animal world. Kangaroos, wallabies, wombats and even birds from near and far came to taste his culinary creations. Kim's Cafe became the talk of the outback.

One day, a little koala named Kobi walks into the cafe. Kobe was known to be a picky eater and rarely tried anything new. Kim gave him a warm welcome and presented him with a special honey drizzled eucalyptus leaf salad. Coby is hesitant but decides to give it a try.

To his surprise, Koby loved it! He ate every bite and even asked for seconds. Kim was thrilled to see how happy her food made Coby.

From that day on, Coby became a regular at Kangaroo Kim's Kangaroo Cafe.

As more animals arrive at Kim's cafe, she continues to create new and exciting dishes. She made gumleaf spaghetti, wildflower pancakes, and even a dessert called "wattleseed delight." Every dish was a hit, and Kim's Cafe became a special place where everyone felt welcome One rainy afternoon, a dingo named Dylan walks into the cafe. Dylan had always been a bit of a troublemaker in the outback and many animals were wary of him. But Kim didn't judge Dylan by his reputation. He greeted her with a smile and offered her a bowl of bush tomato soup.

Dylan was shocked by Kim's kindness. He had never felt such warmth and acceptance before. As he tasted the delicious soup, he realized that he no longer wanted to be a troublemaker. He wanted to change and be a better dingo.

Kim's cafe had a magical effect on all who entered. It wasn't just a place to eat; It was a place where friendships blossomed and hearts were touched. Animals of all kinds gathered together, sharing stories and laughter over Kangaroo Kim's delicious food.

On a sunny day, kangaroos, wallabies and even a couple of wombats decide to put on a concert at the cafe. They sang about the beauty of the outback and the joy of friendship. Music filled the air and animals from all around came to join in the celebration.

Kangaroo Kim's Kangaroo Cafe has become more than just a place to eat; It was the heart and soul of the Outback. It was a place where differences were celebrated, friendships were made and dreams came true.

And so, with her delicious food and her open heart, Kangaroo Kim and her cafe have become legends in the Australian outback, proving that even the simplest ideas, when fueled by love and kindness, can create something truly extraordinary.

Riley's Rainy Day Kangaroo Adventure

Once upon a time in the cozy little town of Willowville, there lived a
curious and adventurous boy named Riley. Riley was known for her
love of exploration and was always looking for new adventures no
matter the weather. One rainy morning, with drops falling on his
window, Riley knew he had to find something exciting.
In a bright yellow raincoat, matching boots, and an umbrella that
looked like it could lift him off the ground, Riley set off into the rainy
day. His mother looked at him with a worried smile as he walked out
the door. "Stay safe, Riley!" He called her.

Riley wandered the damp streets of Willowville and noticed
something unusual in the park.

There was a kangaroo standing under a big oak tree. Not just any
kangaroo, but a kangaroo with the most colorful coat he's ever seen. It
had shades of purple, green and blue and seemed to shimmer in the
rain.
Riley approached the kangaroo cautiously, and said in surprise. "G'day,
mate! I'm Kenny, colored kangaroo," it says in a cheerful Australian
accent.
Riley's eyes widened in surprise. "Can you say?"
Kenny the Kangaroo nodded. "Actually, I can, and I have a special
talent. I bring color to the world, especially on a gray and rainy day like
today."
Riley's face lit up with excitement. "Can you show me, Kenny?"

With a mischievous grin, Kenny hopped around, and as he did, a trail of colorful sparkles followed him. The dull gray environment was transformed into a vibrant, colorful wonderland. The raindrops sparkled like diamonds and the flowers in the park burst into a riot of color.

Riley can't believe her eyes. "That's amazing, Kenny! Can I join you on your adventure?"

Kenny the Kangaroo didn't hesitate. "Sure, mate! Hold on tight!" With a mighty leap, they flew through the rain-drenched air, leaving a trail of rainbows behind them. Riley laughed in pure delight as they bounced from cloud to cloud, exploring the rainy sky.

They visit places Riley never imagined, such as Rainbow Valley, where they slide down colorful slopes, and Crystal Lake, where they watch shimmering fish dance beneath the water's surface. It was the most magical adventure Riley had ever experienced.

As the afternoon wore on, Riley knew it was time to go home. Kenny lands softly in the park, and the vibrant colors begin to fade, returning the world to its rainy gray. Riley sighed, feeling grateful for the wonderful adventure she had shared with Kenny.

"Thanks, Kenny, for showing me beauty on a rainy day," Riley said. Kenny the Kangaroo smiled warmly. "You're welcome, buddy. Remember, there's magic in every moment, even on the rainiest of days."

With one final hop and a wave, Kenny disappeared into the rain. As Riley heads home, her heart is full of gratitude and a new appreciation for rainy days.

From that day on, Riley never let the gloomy weather get her down. Instead, he embraced the rain as an opportunity for new adventures, knowing that somewhere out there, Kenny the Kangaroo of Color was waiting to share another magical journey. And so, in Willowville, every rainy day becomes a day of wonder and excitement for Riley and her colorful friend Kenny.

Kangaroo Kaleb's Kangaroo Quest

Once upon a time, in the vast and sunny Australian outback, there lived a young kangaroo named Caleb.

Caleb was unlike any other kangaroo in his crowd. He was known for his boundless curiosity and adventurous spirit. While his kangaroo friends were content to romp around and crunch through the leaves, Caleb dreamed of big adventures.

One sunny morning, as Caleb was walking through the bushes, he heard a faint cry for help. It sounded like another kangaroo in pain. Without a moment's hesitation, Caleb followed the sound, bounding over bushes and rocks with incredible agility.

Soon, he reached a clearing and found a baby kangaroo or a zoe tangled in a thorn bush. Little Joe's big brown eyes filled with tears, and he couldn't seem to free himself from the prickly predicament.

"Hello there!" Caleb called out, trying to comfort Joy. "Don't worry, I'm here to help."

With gentle care, Caleb used his strong legs and sharp claws to carefully free Joey from the thorns. The little one was grateful and introduced himself as Joey.

"Thanks, Caleb! You're my hero!" Joey said with a grateful smile.

Caleb grinned, feeling proud. "No problem, Joey. I'm always here to help a friend out."

As Caleb and Joey become fast friends, Joey shares a remarkable story. He told Caleb about a legendary treasure hidden deep in the heart of the Outback, which would bring good fortune to those who found it. The treasure was guarded by a wise old kangaroo known as Ru-ru.

Kalb's adventurous spirit flared with excitement. He knew that he had waited all his life for this treasure.

"Joey, we're going on a kangaroo quest to find Roo-Roo and the legendary treasure!" Caleb declared.

Zoya's eyes sparkled with excitement. "I'm with you all the way, Caleb!"

So, the two kangaroos embark on their epic adventure, running through the outback, crossing deserts and jumping rivers. Along the way, they encountered many challenges, from sly dingoes to thorn bushes, but Caleb's determination and Zoe's enthusiasm kept them going.

After days of travel, they finally reach the heart of the Outback, a place where the land glows with a golden glow. There, in the shade of a giant eucalyptus tree, they find Ru-Ru.

Roo-roo was the oldest and wisest kangaroo they had ever met, with a gray coat that glittered like silver. He greeted Caleb and Joey with warm smiles and listened to their stories.

"Little one, the treasure you seek is not gold or jewels," explained Ru-ru. "It is the knowledge that kindness, bravery and friendship are the true treasures of life."

Caleb and Joey were humbled by Roo-roo's intelligence. They realized that their journey had already brought them their greatest treasure—courage, compassion, and unbreakable bonds of friendship.

When they said goodbye to Roo-Roo and headed home, Caleb and Joey knew their adventure had been a success in ways they never imagined. They found the most precious treasure in their hearts.

And so, the kangaroos Caleb and Joey return to their flock, not as heroes of wealth but as heroes of heart, ready to share their incredible journey and the knowledge they have gained with all their kangaroo friends.

From that day on, Caleb and Joey were known as the bravest and kindest kangaroos in the outback, and their quest became a legendary story told to young kangaroos all over the country.

And for Caleb, he realized that the greatest adventures don't always take you far from home but the ones that touch your heart and soul.

And so, Kangaroo Caleb's Kangaroo Quest became a story of kindness, adventure and friendship that would inspire generations of young kangaroos in the Australian outback.

Lily's Kangaroo Kite

Once upon a time in the sunny outback of Australia, there lived a little girl named Lily. He had a big heart and an even bigger imagination. Lily loved spending her days outdoors, exploring the vast and beautiful landscape around her home.

One bright and breezy morning, as Lily was playing in her backyard, she saw a group of kangaroos hopping across the open field. Their long legs and powerful jumps fascinated him, and he couldn't help but wish he could jump as high and far as them.

Lily's father, seeing her fascination, decided to surprise her. He said, "Lily, you want to have your own kangaroo adventure today?"

Lily's eyes sparkled with excitement. "Oh, yes, father! What can we do?"

Baba smiled and brought out a colorful kite from the shed. It was no ordinary kite; It had a picture of a kangaroo on it and was as big as Lily. He handed it to her and said, "This kite will be your kangaroo today. Go to the nearest meadow and see how high it can jump."

Lily's heart danced with joy as she walked to the meadow. The wind was perfect for kite flying, and Lily felt like she had her very own kangaroo by her side. Dad helped him fly the kite in the air and it soared above them.

Lily gripped the kite string tightly, and as she felt the kite pulling towards her, she imagined herself as a kangaroo, ready to jump.

Starting to run, he leapt into the air, his feet barely touching the ground. To his surprise, the kite followed his lead, leaping and dancing in the air.

For hours, Lily and her father played with the kangaroo kite. Like wild kangaroos, they made it jump high and swoop down. The kite seemed to come alive, and Lily giggled with delight as it mimicked the graceful movements of a real kangaroo.

As the day wore on, they attracted the attention of some curious creatures. A flock of colorful birds joined in the fun, kites flew around, and even a friendly wallaby flew in to see what all the excitement was about.

Lily's heart swelled with happiness. She seemed like the luckiest girl in the world, having her own kangaroo adventure right in her backyard. The sun is starting to set, it's time to go home. Lily thanked her father for an incredible day and hugged him tightly. "Dad, this was the best kangaroo adventure ever! I love my kangaroo kite."

Dad smiled warmly. "I'm glad you had so much fun, Lily. Remember, you don't need a real kangaroo to have an adventure. With your imagination and a little magic, you can have a great adventure anytime."

Lily nodded, knowing she would cherish this day forever. He carefully folded his kangaroo kite and put it back in the shed, ready for more adventures in the future.

That night, as Lily lay in her bed, she couldn't help but smile. He knew that even though he couldn't jump like a kangaroo, he had his special kangaroo kite to remind him that adventure and imagination could take him to amazing places. And with that thought, he drifted off to sleep dreaming of his next thrilling adventure in the outback.

Kangaroo Katie's Kangaroo Kart

Once upon a time in the heart of the Australian outback, there lived a young and energetic kangaroo named Katie. Katie was not your ordinary kangaroo; He had a dream, a dream as vast as the wide, open sky above him.

Katie was always fascinated by speed and adventure. While other kangaroos spent their days wandering from place to place, Katie preferred to run with the wind, her long legs carrying her like thunder across the red desert sand.

One sunny morning, Katie was walking around in search of juicy eucalyptus leaves when she saw a group of emus racing each other in their go-karts. They zoomed past him, leaving a trail of dust behind.

Katie's heart leapt with excitement. He had an idea that would make his dream come true. He wanted to build his own kangaroo cart and join Emud in their thrilling race.

Katie gathered her kangaroo friends Billy, Ruby and Sammy to share her exciting plans. They all agreed to help him, and they started brainstorming for the kangaroo cart.

With teamwork and determination, they gathered materials from the outback - a hardwood frame, old tires for the wheels and some spare metal pieces for the cart's body. Katie's friends used their sharp claws to shape the materials while she supervised.

Days turned into weeks and the cart began to take shape. Katie couldn't contain her excitement. He imagined himself speeding across the outback, the wind in his fur and a huge smile on his face.

Finally, after much effort and laughter, the kangaroo cart was ready. It was painted in bright shades of red and yellow, with a kangaroo silhouette on the side. It was a masterpiece, and Katie couldn't be prouder.

The cart had a special feature - a pouch on the back for carrying eucalyptus leaves. That way, Katie can still enjoy her favorite snacks while racing.

Emura was intrigued to hear about Katie's cart. They decided to give him a chance and allowed him to join their next race. Katie was overjoyed and couldn't wait for the big day.

Race day had arrived, and the Outback was buzzing with excitement. Emus and kangaroos from all around gathered to watch the thrilling cart race. Katie jumped into her kangaroo cart, adjusted her goggles and restarted the engine. The race began with a roar! Emu and Katie zoom across the desert, kicking up clouds of dust.

Katie's kart was fast, and she had an incredible knack for maneuvering it around obstacles. He jumped into the air, his strong legs giving him an extra boost and landed gracefully. The crowd cheered as they had never seen a kangaroo race like this before.

The race was neck and neck, but in the final stretch, Katie pushed the pedal to the metal. Speeding, he crossed the finish line just ahead of the fastest emus. He won!

Emura was competitive but gracious in defeat. They congratulate Katie on her incredible racing skills and welcome her to their racing family.

Katie's dream came true. He had his own kangaroo cart, and he proved that kangaroos can be as fast and brave as emus.

From that day, kangaroo kart racing outback became a popular sport. Katie, with her cart, became a legend, and young kangaroos everywhere looked up to her as their hero.

Katie's kangaroo cart was not only a symbol of speed and adventure; It symbolized dreaming big and working hard to make those dreams come true.

And so, Kangaroo Katie's Kangaroo Cart became a beloved story in the outback, inspiring generations of young kangaroos to chase their dreams and stop believing in themselves.

Finn's Fantastic Kangaroo Feat

Once upon a time, in a small Australian town nestled between rolling hills and eucalyptus trees, there lived a young man named Finn. Finn was known for his boundless curiosity and his love for animals. But his favorite animal was the kangaroo. He admired their strong legs and their incredible jumping ability. Finn dreamed of one day having his own kangaroo friend.

One sunny morning, while Finn was exploring the outskirts of town, he stumbled upon a wildlife sanctuary. The sanctuary was home to a variety of Australian animals, including kangaroos. Finn's eyes widened with excitement as he saw kangaroos hopping around in a wide enclosure.

Finn approached Sarah, the sanctuary's friendly ranger, who was feeding the kangaroos. "Wow!

Kangaroos are amazing!" She was startled. "I wish I could jump like them."

Sarah smiled at Finn's enthusiasm. "You know, Finn," he said, "kangaroos are incredible jumpers, but with determination and practice, you can achieve your own great kangaroo feat."

Inspired by Sara's words, Finn decides to learn the art of jumping like a kangaroo. He visited the sanctuary every day after school, watched the kangaroos closely and tried to imitate their movements. At first, his leaps were short, and he often stumbled, but Finn was determined.

Days turned into weeks, and Finn's jumps continued to improve. He practiced tirelessly, jumping and bounding through the field, just as he admired the kangaroos. Sarah and the kangaroos at the sanctuary become his mentors, encouraging him every step of the way.

One bright morning, Finn had a brilliant idea. He decided to organize a kangaroo jumping competition in his town. He knew it would be a fantastic event that would bring the community together and raise awareness of Australian wildlife.

Finn worked hard to prepare for the competition. He designed colorful posters to spread the word about the event. The entire town buzzed with excitement as the kangaroo jumping contest was anticipated.

Finally the day of the competition arrived. The town square was full of eager visitors and the sanctuary's kangaroos were special guests. Finn was ready, dressed in his best kangaroo-themed outfit.

As Finn stood at the starting line, he felt a surge of nervous energy. But then he remembered the encouragement of Sarah and her kangaroo friends. Taking a deep breath he started jumping up and down, just like the kangaroos he had seen so long.

Finn's jump was amazing! He flew into the air, and the crowd cheered with each impressive leap. The other participants were good, but Finn's dedication and practice made him stand out.

In the end, Finn won the kangaroo jumping competition, and his incredible feat earned him a trophy shaped like a kangaroo. But more than that, he fulfilled his dream of jumping like a kangaroo.

Finn's great kangaroo feat inspired the whole town. They realized that with determination and practice they could achieve their dreams too. Wildlife sanctuaries received generous donations, and people began to appreciate and protect Australian wildlife more.

Finn's love of kangaroos and his tenacity not only brought joy to his own life but also had a positive impact on his community and

Australia's precious wildlife. From that day, he knew that dreams can come true if you believe in them and work hard to achieve them.

And so, Finn's fantastic kangaroo feat has become something of a legend in his small Australian town, reminding everyone that even the wildest dreams can come true with dedication and a little pep in their step.

Kangaroo Kyle's Kangaroo Collection

Once upon a time, in the sunny country of Australia, there lived a young kangaroo named Kyle. Kyle was no ordinary kangaroo; He had a deep passion for collecting things. His favorite pastime was collecting all sorts of items from around the bush and he was known far and wide for his unique and extensive collection.

One sunny morning, Kyle woke up with a bright idea. He decided to start a brand new collection, but this time, he wanted it to be extra special. He decided to collect other kangaroos' favorite things. Kyle believed that by doing this, he would learn more about his kangaroo friends and make them feel special.

With his pouch empty and heart full of excitement, Kyle jumps into the bush to find his first item. His first friend was the kangaroo Kevin, a kangaroo who loved coloring pages. Kyle approached Kevin and asked, "Kevin, what's your favorite thing in the whole world?"

Kevin smiled, "I love the colorful leaves, Kyle. They remind me of the beautiful seasons outside here."

Kyle nodded, and with his strong legs he gathered the most beautiful and vibrant leaves he could find. He carefully placed them in his pouch.

Next, Kyle meets Caitlin the kangaroo, who has a passion for shiny pebbles. "Catelyn, does your heart fill with joy?" Kyle asked.

Caitlin smiled and replied, "I love the shiny pebbles, Kyle. They sparkle like the stars at night."

Kyle swarms around and collects pebbles, which reflect the bright sun overhead. They also found a comfortable place in his pouch.

As Kyle continues his search, he meets the kangaroo Kelsey, who is fascinated by seashells. "Kelsey, what's your favorite treasure?" Kyle asked.

Kelsey smiled, "I'm fascinated by seashells, Kyle. They remind me of beaches and calm waves."

Kyle went to a nearby creek, where he found the most exquisite seashells, each with a unique pattern and color. He carefully collects them.

Finally, Kyle encounters Krista the kangaroo, who has a love for colorful flowers. "Christa, what makes your heart bounce?" Kyle asked.

Christa blushed and replied, "I'm fascinated by colorful flowers, Kyle. They fill the air with joy."

Kyle gathered the most vibrant flowers from around the bush, making sure to leave some for the bees and butterflies.

His pouch now filled with leaves, pebbles, seashells and flowers, Kyle felt delighted. He had collected his kangaroo friends' favorite things, and he knew it was time to share his collection with them.

Kyle walked back to where his friends were and presented each of them with their favorite items.

Kangaroo Kevin, Kaitlyn, Kelsey and Krista were delighted and touched by Kyle's thoughtful gesture.

As the kangaroos admire their gifts, Kyle realizes that his collection has become even more special as it brings joy to his friends. And so, he continues to collect not only things, but also the smiles of his kangaroo companions.

Since that day, Kangaroo Kyle became known not only for his impressive collection, but also for his kind heart and ability to bring joy to those around him. And as the kangaroos bounded through the Australian outback, they knew their friendship and shared happiness were the most valuable treasures.

Sophie's Secret Kangaroo Garden

Once upon a time, in a small town on the edge of a vast and dusty outback, lived a young woman named Sophie. Sophie was an adventurous and imaginative child who loved exploring the wonders of nature. His favorite animals in the world were kangaroos, with their long legs and bouncy hops. He often dreams of seeing a close up.

One sunny morning, while Sophie was playing in her backyard, she had an idea. He decided to build a secret kangaroo garden. With a blink of her eye, she gathered her gardening tools and began her mission.

Sophie dug a large hole in a sunny corner of the yard, deep enough to plant the special kangaroo seed she got from her grandmother. These seeds were said to grow in the habitat of a magical kangaroo. Sophie planted them carefully, watered them and gave them all the love and attention they needed.

The days turned into weeks, and Sophie watched with anticipation as the kangaroo garden began to bloom. First came tall, green grass, perfect for kangaroos. Next, colorful flowers bloom, attracting butterflies and bees.

One evening, as the sun was setting, Sophie heard a soft rustling sound coming from the garden. As he got closer he couldn't believe his eyes - a baby kangaroo, known as a joey, came out from behind the bush. Sophie's heart skipped a beat with joy.

He names little Joey Joey, and the two quickly become inseparable friends. Sophie spent her afternoons reading stories to Joey, who listened intently, as if understanding every word. They played tag and hide and seek, and Joey even taught Sophie how to run like a kangaroo.

As the days turn into months, Sophie's secret kangaroo garden becomes a magical place for more kangaroos. Word spread among the kangaroo families outside and they regularly visited Sophie's garden. They jumped around, frolicked on the grass and played together under the warm Australian sun.

Sophie's garden was a place of laughter and joy, where humans and kangaroos coexisted peacefully. Sophie's parents marveled at their daughter's secret garden and often sat on the balcony watching the kangaroos with smiles on their faces.

One day, Sophie decides to share her secret with her best friend Mia. He took Mia to the garden, where they both watched in awe as the kangaroos frolicked and played. Sophie explains how she planted the magical seed, and Mia can't believe what she's seeing.

Word spread, and soon, the whole town came to see Sophie's magical kangaroo garden. It becomes a place of wonder and enchantment for all. Sophie's garden was no longer a secret, but it was still a special place filled with love and laughter.

As the years pass, Sophie and Joey continue to grow together and their bond becomes stronger than ever. The garden remains a symbol of the incredible friendship between man and nature.

And so, Sophie's secret kangaroo garden brings happiness not only to her but to an entire community, teaching them the beauty and magic of friendship to be found in the natural world, right in their own backyard.

the end

Kangaroo Kaitlyn's Kangaroo Cabaret

Once upon a time in the heart of the Australian outback, there lived a young kangaroo named
Caitlin. Caitlin was known for her extraordinary talent – she could jump higher and dance better than any other kangaroo in the entire Outback. But Caitlin had a dream. She didn't just want to dance for herself; She wanted to share her love for dance with everyone.
One sunny morning, Caitlin approached her best friend Joey the wallaby with an exciting idea. "Joey, I want to make a kangaroo cabaret!" he exclaimed.
Joy's eyes sparkled with curiosity. "A kangaroo cabaret? What is it, Caitlin?"
Kaitlin explained her concept, "This is a show where we kangaroos showcase our unique talents dancing, singing and even magic tricks! And the best part, everyone is welcome to join in and have fun!"
Joey laughed, "That sounds amazing, Caitlin! Let's do it!"
Kaitlyn and Joey start spreading the word about their Kangaroo Cabaret. They made colorful flyers and invited kangaroos from all over the outback to join the fun. It didn't take long for all ages to sign Up for Kangaroo Cabaret. Some could dance, some could sing, and some had tricks up their sleeves.
Caitlin worked tirelessly to organize the cabaret. He found a perfect spot in a grassy clearing surrounded by eucalyptus trees. He and Joey built a stage using logs and painted a big, bright banner that read, "Kangaroo Caitlin's Kangaroo Cabaret."

As the day of Cabaret approached, excitement filled the air. The kangaroos practiced their routines and fine-tuned their performances. Kaitlyn choreographed a special dance number that she would perform with Zoe and it was the talk of the outback.

Finally, the day arrived. Kangaroos and other animals from near and far flocked to the cabaret grounds. Caitlin looked out at the crowd, her heart filled with joy. He was going to make his dream come true.

The cabaret began with a lively dance number by a group of kangaroos. They jumped to the beat of the music as the audience cheered. Then, there were singers who hummed beautiful tunes, and even a magical kangaroo whose colorful scarves disappeared and reappeared!

As the sun began to set, it was time for Kaitlyn's special dance with Joey. They ran gracefully across the stage, their moves perfectly synchronized. The audience was mesmerized by their performance, and they received a standing ovation.

But Kaitlyn had one more surprise up her furry sleeve. He invited the youngest kangaroos from the crowd to join them on stage. Together, they danced to a catchy tune, their tiny feet bouncing in pure joy. It was a heartwarming moment, and the entire outdoor community came together in celebration.

Kangaroo Cabaret became a huge success, just as Caitlin had dreamed. The kangaroos laughed, danced and shared their talents with each other and it became an annual tradition in the Outback. Caitlin's dream of sharing her love of dancing came true, and she was the happiest kangaroo in the entire wide outback.

From that day forward, the Kangaroo Cabaret continues to bring happiness to the Outback, reminding everyone that dreams can come true, as long as you have the courage to chase them, just like Caitlin the Kangaroo.

Tommy's Tumbling Kangaroo

Once upon a time, in the heart of the Australian outback, lived a little boy named Tommy. Tommy had always dreamed of an adventure, but he didn't know where to find it. He lived on a farm with his parents and spent most of his days helping with the work and playing with the farm animals.

One sunny morning, while Tommy was feeding the chickens, he heard a strange noise from the nearby bushes. It sounded like a mixture of laughter and jumping. Intrigued, he followed the sound until he stumbled upon the most amazing sight he had ever seen: a kangaroo, but not just any kangaroo—a kangaroo that was tumbling through the air and doing somersaults!

Tommy couldn't believe his eyes. Kangaroos were known for their leaps, not their tumbling. He watched in awe as the kangaroo continued to perform its incredible acrobatics.

The kangaroo noticed Tommy and pounced on him. "G'day, mate! I'm Kip, the tumbling kangaroo," it said with a cheerful smile.

Tommy still blinked. "Wow, Kip! I've never seen a kangaroo do such an amazing trick before. How did you learn to jerk like that?"

Kip laughed, "Well, Tommy, I always like to try new things and push my limits. One day, I decided to see if I could do a somersault, and I kept practicing until I got really good at it. !"

Tommy's face lit up with excitement. "That's incredible, Kip! I wish I could learn to do something so amazing."

Kip thought for a moment. "You know, Tommy, I could teach you some basic tumbling moves. It's a lot of fun, and who knows, maybe you'll discover a talent you didn't know you had!"

Tommy's heart fluttered with joy. "Yes, please, Kip! I want to learn."

And so, Tommy's adventure began. Every day, after he finished his work, he would meet Kip in the bush and they would practice rolling together. Kip taught Tommy how to roll, flip and even do a cartwheel. Tommy was a quick learner and he loved every moment of their training.

Word of Tommy and Kip's tumbling adventure soon spread throughout the Outback. The other animals came to watch them practice and they cheered Tommy on. Even a wise old koala named Charlie came to offer his advice.

As the days turned into weeks, Tommy's skills improved and he became known as "Tommy the Tumbling Boy". He was no longer just a farm boy; He was a local legend. But what mattered most to Tommy was the incredible bond he formed with Kip, the kangaroo.

One day, while Tommy and Kip were practicing their most daring moves, they heard a loud cry for help from a nearby hill. It was a baby wallaby stuck on a narrow ledge. Without thinking, Tommy and Kip rush to the rescue. Tommy uses his newfound tumbling skills to reach the baby wallaby and bring it down to safety.

A grateful wallaby mother thanked Tommy and Kip. Word of their adventure spread far and wide, and Tommy became a hero not only in the Outback, but throughout Australia.

Tommy realized that sometimes, the most incredible adventures can be found right in your own backyard. He also learned that when you follow your passion and work hard, you can achieve amazing things, just like he did with Tumble.

And so, Tommy continues to hang out with the keep, sharing their skills and joy with everyone they meet. Together, they showed the world that even a boy from a small farm could achieve great heights with a little determination and a lot of friendship.

From that day on, whenever anyone asked Tommy how he found his adventure, he would simply laugh and say, "I got into it with the help of a kangaroo named Kip." And they all went through life's adventures together and lived happily ever after.

the end

Kangaroo Kara's Kangaroo Circus

Once upon a time, in the heart of the Australian outback, lived a young and adventurous kangaroo named Kara. Kara was no ordinary kangaroo; He had a dream as big as the vast desert. Kara wanted to create a spectacular circus, but not just any circus - a kangaroo circus! Kara believed that kangaroos were the best jumpers in the world, and she wanted to showcase their incredible talent to everyone. He knew that if he could gather a team of talented kangaroos, his dream could come true.

One sunny morning, Kara went up to her friends den to share her dream. There was Kenny, a kangaroo known for his incredible high jumps, Ruby, the fastest kangaroo in the outback, and Benny, who was the best at balancing on his tail. Kara explained her plan, and her friends couldn't be more excited.

Together, they set off to find more kangaroos who can join their circus. They traveled through dusty deserts, over mountains and across rivers. Along the way, they met Kylie, who could do somersaults in the air, and Zoe, who had an amazing talent for spinning. The group grows larger and more talented with each new friend they meet.

After many days of searching, they finally found enough kangaroos to build Kangaroo Kara's Kangaroo Circus. Kara was overjoyed, but she knew there was still a lot of work to be done. They needed a big top tent, colorful banners and a special place for the audience to sit.

With determination and teamwork, they gather materials and build the circus from scratch.

Cara and her friends painted the banners with vibrant colors, and they created a magical spotlight using the moon's reflection. The stage was set, and Kangaroo Kara's Kangaroo Circus was ready to make its grand debut.

News of the kangaroo circus quickly spread across the Outback and all manner of animals came to see the incredible show. Kara and her friends wowed the audience with their breathtaking performances.

Kenny jumped so high he looked up to the sky. Ruby ran around the ring in a blur, surprising everyone. Benny gracefully balanced on his tail, and

Kylie's somersault brought cheers from the crowd. Joey is faster and taller than anyone can imagine.

As the moon rises in the night sky, the circus reaches its grand finale.

Kara and her friends, joined by all the other kangaroos, jump in unison, creating a mesmerizing kangaroo dance in the moonlight. It was a sight to behold and the audience cheered and clapped for joy. Kangaroo Cara's Kangaroo Circus not only entertained the outback but also inspired others to follow their dreams. Kara and her friends were happy and full of pride. Their dream came true, and it was even more incredible than they had imagined.

And so, in the heart of the Australian outback, Kangaroo Kara's Kangaroo Circus has come to symbolize the pursuit of dreams, teamwork and the amazing talent of kangaroos. Kara and her friends continued their circus, bringing joy and wonder to those who watched, and they knew that as long as they had each other, their dreams would always be as high as kangaroos can jump.

Max's Marvelous Kangaroo Map

Once upon a time, in a sunny little town called Hopesville, there lived a curious and adventurous boy named Max. Max was known throughout Hopesville for his love of exploration and his trusty backpack, filled with all sorts of exciting gadgets and tools. But what he loved most was maps. Max has collected all types of maps from pirate treasure maps to ancient world maps.

One day, while exploring the attic of his grandmother's house, Max stumbles upon an old, dusty map. It was unlike any other he had ever seen before. There was a kangaroo on the map, and Max was surprised. He had never heard of kangaroos living in Hopesville. His grandmother, who was knitting in the corner, noticed Max's fascination with the map and smiled.

"This is a very special map, Max," she said. "It's been in our family for generations. Legend has it that it leads to a hidden kangaroo kingdom deep in the heart of the outback."

Max's eyes widened in excitement. He couldn't believe his luck. He decided right then and there that he was going to find this hidden kangaroo kingdom. His grandmother had given him the map, which was fragile and yellow with age. "Careful, Max," she warned. "The journey won't be easy, but I trust you."

Max spent the next few days preparing for his adventure. He documented his journey with snacks, water, a compass and a camera in his backpack. The map was now his most prized possession and he guarded it carefully.

One morning, Max sets out on his quest. He followed the winding path on the map, crossing rivers and climbing steep hills. Along the way, he encounters many curious animals such as wallabies, emus and even a friendly kookaburra who laugh at his jokes. Max kept his spirits high knowing the kangaroo kingdom was waiting for him.

After days of traveling through the vast and beautiful outback, Max finally arrives at a clearing. He couldn't believe his eyes. In front of him was a huge rock formation that looked like a kangaroo and had a hidden entrance at its base.

Max entered the Kangaroo Kingdom with a heart full of excitement. Inside, he finds a magical world filled with kangaroos of all shapes and colors. They welcome Max with warm smiles and invite him to join their daily kangaroo game. Max jumped up and down with them, feeling like one of the kangaroo clan.

As days turned into weeks, Max learned about the lifestyle of kangaroos. They share stories of their ancestors and teach Max about the importance of protecting their home, the outback. Max was inspired by their wisdom and love of their land.

Finally, Max knew it was time to return to Hopesville. The kangaroos gave him a special kangaroo pouch as a token of their friendship and promise to protect the outback. With a heavy heart, Max left the Kangaroo Kingdom, but he knew he would return one day.

When Max returns to Hopesville, he shares his incredible adventure with his family and friends.

He shows them the kangaroo pouch and explains the importance of protecting the environment. Max's story has inspired everyone in Hopesville to take better care of their surroundings.

Max's love of maps has continued since that day, but the Kangaroo Kingdom map holds a special place in his heart. He knew that some treasures were more precious than gold, and the friendships he made in the outback were the most wonderful treasures of all.

And so, Max's extraordinary kangaroo map became a symbol of adventure, friendship and the importance of protecting our planet for generations to come.

Kangaroo Kody's Kangaroo Craft

Once upon a time, in a vast and colorful Australian outback, there lived a young kangaroo named Cody. Cody was not like other kangaroos who enjoyed hanging out and playing games all day. Cody had a unique passion - crafting. Cody loved making things with his little paws and had a special place in his heart for making beautiful crafts. His pouch was always filled with colorful papers, glitter, glue, and all sorts of odds and ends found during his adventures. He often collected shiny pebbles, beautiful leaves and twigs that he believed could be transformed into something magical.

One sunny morning, as Cody sat under a gum tree, he noticed his friends excitedly discussing the upcoming annual Outback Talent Show. They were planning to show off their amazing hooping skills and tell the story of their adventures. Cody was a bit left out because he couldn't run like them, but he had an idea.

She fumbled (well, sort of skipped) over to her bag and pulled out a piece of colored paper, some twigs, and her trusty bottle of glitter. Cody was going to create a craft that would not only amaze his friends but also make him the star of the talent show.

Cody began working on his project with all his heart. He carefully cut out a kangaroo shape using colored paper. He added twigs for legs and his little paws worked to quickly glue them in place. The finishing touch was a sprinkling of glitter to make her craft sparkle in the sunshine outside.

As the days passed, Cody worked tirelessly on his kangaroo craft. He poured his love, creativity and imagination into every detail. He even made a small boomerang out of a branch and painted it with bright colors.

Finally the day of the talent show came. Cody nervously took the stage with his craft in his arms. When it was his turn, he proudly presented his masterpiece to the cheering crowd.

His friends gasped in awe at the incredible kangaroo craft. The glitter sparkled, and the kangaroo looked like it could jump right off the paper. Cody explained how he can't run like others, but he poured all his love for kangaroos into creating this work of art.

The crowd was inspired by Cody's dedication and creativity. They applauded him for his unique talent and Cody felt a warm glow of joy inside him. He realized that it was not for high or far; It was about being true to oneself and making one happy.

Cody's kangaroo craft won everyone's hearts at the talent show and he received a special award for his exceptional creativity. From that day on, he was known as "Cratty Cody" in the Outback and his craft creations brought smiles to the faces of all his friends.

Cody's story taught other kangaroos an important lesson: everyone had their own special talents and strengths. The annual talent show no longer focuses solely on hopping; It celebrated all kinds of talent from singing to storytelling to crafts.

And so, in the vast and colorful Australian outback, Cody's passion for craft helps his friends discover their own unique talents, making their world a brighter and happier place.

Since then, Crafty Kody has spent her days creating beautiful crafts, spreading joy, and inspiring others to embrace their passions and share their unique gifts with the world. And he continued to craft, hop and sparkle under the warm sun of the Australian outback, knowing that being true to himself was the most beautiful talent.

Olivia's Outback Kangaroo Adventure

Once upon a time, in a sunny land far away, there lived a young woman named Olivia. Olivia has always dreamed of exploring the great Australian outback, a vast wilderness filled with unique animals and stunning landscapes. His parents often told him stories about the fascinating animals that call the outback their home, especially kangaroos.

One bright morning, Olivia wakes up with an idea that fills her heart with excitement. He decided it was time to embark on the adventure of a lifetime and meet the famous kangaroos of the outback. He packs his backpack with some snacks, water and a trusty map his parents gave him.

With determination and a sense of curiosity, Olivia begins her journey. The outback was a vast, wild place, but Olivia wasn't afraid. He followed his map carefully, making his way along the red, dusty path.

As the day progresses, Olivia sees a variety of animals native to the Outback. He saw colorful parrots with vibrant feathers and friendly wallabies roaming around. But he was still in search of the kangaroo, the star of his adventure.

After walking for hours, Olivia notices a group of kangaroos in the distance. His heart raced with joy! He approached them carefully, not wanting to startle them. The kangaroos looked at her with their big, curious eyes and Olivia couldn't help but smile.

Olivia sat quietly and watched the kangaroos go about their day. He watched them leap effortlessly across the open plain, their powerful hind legs propelling them forward. It was a mesmerizing sight and Olivia felt like she was in a dream.

One kangaroo, in particular, caught Olivia's attention. He was a little joey, still a baby kangaroo, and seemed to have trouble keeping up with the older kangaroos. Olivia decided to call him Joey.

With a gentle look, Olivia offered Joey a piece of her food. At first, she was a bit shy, but eventually, she took the treat from his hand. Olivia giggled in delight, and from that moment on, she and Joey became fast friends.

As the day turned to evening, Olivia realized it was time to go home. He bids farewell to the kangaroos, including Joey, promising to meet them again soon. With a happy heart and a new love for the outback, Olivia returns to her own home.

Over the next few months, Olivia visits the outback many times, always returning to her kangaroo friends. He learned a lot about their habits, their families and their incredible ability to adapt to the wild environment. Olivia even started a journal to document her adventures and shared them with her family and friends.

Olivia's outback kangaroo adventures have become legendary in her town. He inspired other kids to explore the natural wonders in their own backyards, just like he did. And he knew that his friendship with Joey and the kangaroos was something he would cherish forever.

As Olivia grew up, her love for the outback and its kangaroos never wavered. He became a wildlife conservationist, working tirelessly to protect unique animals and their habitats. Olivia's adventures taught her that the world was full of wonders, waiting to be discovered by those with open hearts and curious minds.

And so, Olivia's outback kangaroo adventure becomes a story that will inspire generations to come, reminding them of the magic that awaits those who dare to explore the world around them.

Kangaroo Kevin's Kangaroo Magic

Once upon a time, in the vast and sunny outback of Australia, there lived a young kangaroo named Kevin. Kevin was a normal kangaroo like all the other kangaroos in his family. He had soft, brown fur, long, strong legs and a big, bouncy tail. But Kevin was different in a special way - he believed in magic.

Kevin was always fascinated by magical stories, where everything was possible. He dreamed of performing magic tricks just like the magicians he saw on television. He spent his days wandering around the outback, collecting sticks, leaves and colored stones, which he believed were magical ingredients.

One sunny morning, while walking through a eucalyptus forest, Kevin finds a shiny, old book hidden under a tree stump. It was covered in dust and read in golden letters "The Book of Kangaroo Magic." Kevin's heart raced with excitement as he opened the book.

Inside, he discovered all kinds of spells and tricks. There were spells to make the sun shine brighter, tricks to make flowers bloom instantly, and even spells to make water sparkle like diamonds. Kevin was very happy; He found his own magic book!

He decided to practice his new magical skills. The first spell he cast was to create a field of wildflowers. He hopped into a nearby meadow, whispered magical words and waved his paw. To his surprise, the field burst into all kinds of colorful flowers - red, yellow and blue! Kevin's mind swelled with joy.

Word of Kevin's magic quickly spread to the other kangaroos. Soon, a group of curious kangaroo friends gather around him, asking him to teach him his magical ways. Kevin happily agreed.

Together, they practiced spells to make rainbows appear after rain, light up the night sky with stars, and even create a magical playground with bouncy mushrooms and flying swings. The kangaroos were amazed by their newfound powers and realized that believing in magic made their world a better place.

One day, as Kevin and his kangaroo friends practice their magic by dancing rainbows across the sky, they hear a faint cry for help. They hurried towards the sound and discovered a family of koalas clinging to a tall tree branch. The koalas climbed too high and could not come down.

Without hesitation, Kevin and his friends used their magic to create a soft, fluffy cloud under the tree. The koalas jumped to safety on the clouds and floated down to the ground. Grateful koalas thank Kevin and his kangaroo friends for their incredible magic.

From that day on, Kevin and his friends continued to use their magic to help others in need.

They brought joy to the creatures of the outback and their magical adventures brought them closer as friends.

Kangaroo Kevin discovered that real magic was not in mantras or tricks but in kindness, friendship and the belief that anything is possible if you have a big heart.

And so, in the heart of the Australian outback, kangaroo Kevin and his kangaroo friends lived happily sharing their kangaroo magic with everyone they met.

Lucy and the Kangaroo Carnival

Once upon a time, in a small town in the heart of Australia lived a curious and adventurous girl named Lucy. Lucy was known throughout town for her bright blue eyes and her insatiable curiosity. But the one he loved the most was the kangaroo. He had posters of them on his
bedroom wall, read books about them, and even had a small collection of kangaroo toys.

One sunny morning, Lucy's father surprises her with exciting news. He had heard the kangaroo carnival was coming to town and he knew how much Lucy adored kangaroos. "Lucy," he said with a smile, "we're going to the kangaroo carnival today!"

Lucy's heart leapt for joy. He rushes to get ready in his favorite kangaroo t-shirt and a hat decorated with kangaroo ears. He couldn't wait to see the kangaroos up close and learn more about them.

Lucy's eyes widened in surprise as they arrived at the carnival. There were stalls full of delicious cotton candy, colorful balloons and all kinds of games. But it was the kangaroo exhibit that attracted his most attention.

First they visited the Kangaroo Education Tent. There was a kind and knowledgeable ranger named Mr. Roberts giving a lecture about kangaroos. Lucy listened intently as Mr. Roberts shared interesting facts about kangaroos' lives in the wild. He learned about their powerful legs, their incredible leaping ability, and their pouches in which they carried their young.

After the talk, Lucy couldn't wait to meet some real kangaroos. They went to the kangaroo petting area. The kangaroos were docile and friendly, and Lucy got the chance to stroke their soft fur and feed them some kangaroo snacks. I felt like the luckiest girl in the world. Next, they visited the Kangaroo Art Station, where Lucy got to create her own kangaroo-themed artwork. He painted a beautiful picture of a kangaroo leaping across a vast outback landscape. Lucy was proud of her masterpiece.

As the day progressed, Lucy and her family enjoyed the carnival rides and games. They even won a kangaroo stuffed animal at the game booth. Lucy held it close, feeling a deep connection to this amazing creature.

As the sun begins to set, Lucy's father takes her to the main stage, where a spectacular kangaroo show is about to begin. Kangaroos of all sizes bound the stage, displaying their agility and grace. They jumped, skipped and syncopated to the music leaving the audience in awe. Lucy clapped and cheered with all her might, her heart filled with joy. She never imagined she could have such an incredible day, surrounded by the animals she loved so much.

Finally, as the carnival ends, Lucy reluctantly says goodbye to the kangaroos. He knew he would cherish this day forever. When they returned home, Lucy felt tired but satisfied.

That night, Lucy went to sleep with a smile on her face, her new kangaroo stuffed animal by her side. In his dream, he ran away with the kangaroos he met at the carnival, knowing that his love for these amazing animals would stay with him forever.

And so, in small-town Australia, Lucy's heart was forever attached to the kangaroos she loved, thanks to the magical day she spent at the Kangaroo Carnival.

Milton Keynes UK
Ingram Content Group UK Ltd.
UKHW020723290923
429627UK00015B/707